4/2/13
#35.00

MARSHAL REDLEAF

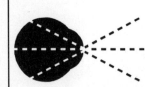

This Large Print Book carries the Seal of Approval of N.A.V.H.

MARSHAL REDLEAF

LAURAN PAINE

THORNDIKE PRESS
A part of Gale, Cengage Learning

GALE
CENGAGE Learning·

Detroit • New York • San Francisco • New Haven, Conn • Waterville, Maine • London

GALE
CENGAGE Learning

Copyright © 2011 by Mona Paine.
Thorndike Press, a part of Gale, Cengage Learning.

Thorndike Press® Large Print Western.
The text of this Large Print edition is unabridged.
Other aspects of the book may vary from the original edition.
Set in 16 pt. Plantin.

LIBRARY OF CONGRESS CATALOGING-IN-PUBLICATION DATA

Paine, Lauran.
   Marshal Redleaf / by Lauran Paine. — Large Print edition.
      pages cm. — (Thorndike Press Large Print Western)
   ISBN-13: 978-1-4104-5679-3 (hardcover)
   ISBN-10: 1-4104-5679-X (hardcover)
   1. Stagecoach robberies—Fiction. 2. Evidence—Fiction. 3. Large type books. I. Title.
   PS3566.A34M37 2013
   813'.54—dc23   2012047519

Published in 2013 by arrangement with Golden West Literary Agency

Printed in the United States of America
1 2 3 4 5 6 7 17 16 15 14 13

MARSHAL REDLEAF

I

Chet Redleaf held the cards against his chest, leaned across the table, and spoke in a low voice. The room was hazy with smoke, there were four other tables, all occupied by card players, some having poker sessions, at least one set of four gamblers engrossed in blackjack, and toward the rear of the card room where lamplight barely reached three swarthy muleteers, who spoke rarely, were playing pedro.

Redleaf said: "There was no leather behind the hub."

His companion glanced up briefly, then returned to the study of his cards. "There usually ain't when that happens."

Redleaf eased back, eyeing his friend. "Lester, when they wear out and you pull a wheel, there is something left. A torn piece of leather, a little ball of it mixed in the grease."

His adversary folded his cards, placed them face down before speaking, and studied the even features across from him — the very dark hair and eyes, the softly bronzed skin — and faintly, sardonically smiled.

"What are you trying to do? Chet, being town marshal don't make you a Pinkerton man." Lester, who was powerfully built, was about the same age as Town Marshal Redleaf, but with Irish blue eyes, carroty-colored hair, and a slightly tipped nose. He sat, gazing across the table. "Nothing happened. The stage burned out a hub and warped an axle. It got here on a wobble. Chet, if there ever was a grease retainer, it just purely got chewed up and spit out along with the grease." Lester Riley reached for his cards. He'd had his say and he thought the topic closed.

The marshal fanned his cards, glanced at them, then looked up to say: "They told me over at the corral yard a leather was put into each wheel two weeks back."

"All right. So one leather was maybe neck or belly leather. Did you have 'em take off the other three wheels?"

"Yes, all the other leathers were in place and showed almost no wear.

Lester, there wasn't any leather put into that fourth wheel."

Riley looked up, annoyed. "All right. Somebody over there forgot and didn't want to admit it and get fired, so he lied. What the hell difference does it make?" Lester shrugged powerful shoulders. "The stage company'll have to buy a new axle, maybe a new wheel or hub. Are we going to play cards or not?"

Marshal Redleaf said nothing. They dealt about six or eight hands with the pots going one way, then the other way. Those swarthy muleteers left and about a half hour later one of the poker sessions also broke up. Its players had all been local cowmen. They nodded to the town marshal on their way toward the heavy red drapery that separated the card room from the saloon.

Lester Riley raked in a pot worth 60¢ and smiled across the table. "That old man who runs the livery barn's going to be waiting up for me."

"Why? Didn't you put your horses in the public corrals?"

"Yeah. But I bought hay and grain from him, and I know him from years back. He can't sleep if someone owes him money."

Redleaf critically examined his cards as he said: "He must use a lot of coal oil then, Les."

"I'll guess. You got four aces?"

"No."

"Four kings. Four of something?"

Redleaf placed a mongrel hand face up for his friend to see, waited until the last players from the nearest table had departed, then said: "I'll tell you why I keep coming back to that missing grease retainer."

Riley was gazing at the worthless hand, three horizontal wrinkles across his broad, low forehead. "You didn't have anything," he eventually said, and leaned back still looking puzzled.

Redleaf ignored his friend's expression. "There is something I didn't tell you."

Riley's voice was flat with annoyance as he said: "What?"

"The stage was six miles north of town when the wheel began smoking and wobbling."

Riley threw up his hands and leaned to rise. He looked thoroughly disgusted.

The town marshal acted as though he had seen none of this. "There were no passengers, just the whip and a young buck the company's training to drive."

"Chet, damn it, everyone knows that."

"Sure. I'll tell you something they don't know. While the whip and his helper were hoisting the near side to take the wheel off to examine the damage, the box of light freight inside the coach on the floor disappeared."

Les Riley gazed steadily at his companion. "Disappeared? A crate of light freight? Where was it to be delivered?"

"To Manion's General Store here in Mandan."

"What d'you mean . . . disappeared? How could anything disappear out of a stagecoach when there were two men pulling a wheel?"

Chet leaned back, too. The card

room was empty. Even the fragrant tobacco smoke was dissipating. "It was there when they stopped. When they were putting up their tools, it was gone. Someone was in the rocks or trees on the offside and, when they were straining to lift the wheel to block it up, sneaked down from the offside, opened the door over there, and took the box."

Riley did not seem entirely convinced anything like that had happened, but he did not dispute it. He instead asked a pointed question: "Why should someone want to steal a box coming here to Manion's? Maybe they'd make off with some corsets, a lady's button shoes, or maybe a box full of that dry oatmeal folks mix with milk and feed to babies."

Redleaf said: "They made off with four thousand dollars in greenbacks." Riley started in his chair. His eyes sprang wide open. For half a minute he sat, staring. Realization, at least a theory, settled in his mind as he loosened in the chair again. "Rodney Manion was trying to sneak four thousand dollars down to Mandan mislabeled as fry pans or something?"

Chet barely inclined his head, and Riley reddened. "That old skinflint. Too cheap to hire an armed guard or outriders." Riley was not fond of the General Store's proprietor. Not very many people were in the Mandan Valley country.

Marshal Redleaf carefully fashioned a rice-paper cigarette and lighted it while waiting for his friend to recover from both shock and indignation. He trickled smoke while eyeing Riley's high color and smoldering gaze. When Riley was about to launch into additional denunciations, the lawman held up his hand with the quirly in it.

"All right. He tried to save money and be clever at the same time and it didn't work. He's going to regret it for the rest of his life. But that's his end of it. My end of it is that there's no other lawman in the area. Also, where the box disappeared was beyond the town limits but well within my operating range."

"Whoa," Riley said softly. "Your authority doesn't extend beyond Mandan's town limits."

Redleaf did not dispute this, he simply stated what had been a recognized fact of life west of the Missouri

River since before either he or Lester Riley had been born. When town marshals were the only duly elected and authorized lawmen in a countryside, if people knew of the limitations they were not supposed to exceed, they neither mentioned it, nor neglected to run for a town marshal any time a law had been broken, and usually in areas miles beyond the legal limits of a town marshal.

Redleaf said: "How long have we known each other?"

Riley's eyes narrowed. "Since I first hauled freight into Mandan. Wait a minute, Chet, I know what you're thinking. I've got some freight to haul out of Mandan for the blacksmith. I've been loafing in Mandan for two weeks but that's about over. I'll be hauling out in a day or two, so I can't help you."

Redleaf began counting the loose silver in front of him on the table. Riley watched this in silence until Redleaf had pocketed his winnings and leaned to rise as he said: "How much did you rake in?"

Riley moved coins before answering. "Lost two dollars and thirty cents. You?"

"Two dollars and thirty cents to the good. Come on, winner stands a round."

When they got out to the bar, most of the patrons had departed earlier. What remained were a sprinkling of range men, a few strangers, probably passing through and stranded in Mandan until the morning stage left town tomorrow, and some townsmen, probably unmarried men.

The barman was a large, massive, beetle-browed individual named Jack Hudson whose normal amiability concealed a temper local saloon patrons knew better than to incite. He winked at Riley and Redleaf, set up a bottle with two jolt glasses, and leaned to watch the lawman pour as he said: "Maybe one of those epidemics is settling in." At the quizzical looks he got for leaving that statement hanging in mid-air, Hudson leaned lower and spoke so softly his words did not carry ten feet. "Joe Manion was taken down sick and had to go home to bed. His clerk said he was red as a beet, didn't hear when someone spoke to him, and wiped tears from his eyes with shaky hands. I looked up them symptoms in my *Doctor Sunday*'s medical book.

19

Seemed to me they fit the signs of cholera, or maybe tick fever, or possibly the bloody flux or lung fever."

Redleaf pushed the bottle away and leaned comfortably while holding his little glass. "I don't think it's catching," he told Jack Hudson, tilted his head, dropped the whiskey straight down, and remained rigid, eyes fixed unblinkingly dead ahead until the almost overpowering urge to shudder from head to heels had passed, then he let go with a long, silent breath of inflammable air and leaned against the bar.

Jack Hudson smiled. "One-third Indian ain't real Indian, is it? A full-blood or even a half-breed would have had tears down his face, he would have been suckin' air like a whale out of water, an' he'd have been grippin' the bar with all his strength."

It was exactly for this reason Chet Redleaf went through his act of iron self-control every time he drank straight whiskey.

Lester Riley had no inhibitions. After downing his jolt, he panted, swore, brushed water from his eyes with the back of a hairy hand, and glared at Jack Hudson. "Where did you get that whiskey?" he asked.

Hudson straightened back, groped beneath the bar, brought up a brown bottle, turned it so lamplight fell across the label, and read aloud: " 'Green River Whiskey. Distilled at Green River, Wyoming by the Green River Fermentation and Bottling Works.' "

Hudson put the bottle in his hand

21

beside the bottle Redleaf and Riley had poured from, and pointed out that they were identical. He also said: "That there is Mormon whiskey."

Riley glared. "Mormons don't make whiskey. They don't drink it, neither. Well, they're not supposed to drink it."

Hudson showed big strong, even white teeth in a bleak grin. "Mister Riley, they make it. This here is genuine Mormon whiskey. The feller who passes through a couple times a year delivering it is a Mormon. Maybe a jack Mormon, but still a Mormon."

They paid for the whiskey, went out into the softly warm springtime night, and stood breathing deeply of air as clear as glass while looking up and down Mandan's main thoroughfare.

Les Riley was still slightly breath-less. "Maybe the Mormons're trying to kill us non-Mormons, Chet."

Marshal Redleaf laughed. "You won't have to worry. You'll be haul-ing out of the territory in a few days. Good night, Les."

"Good night, Chet. I'll look you up when I pass through next time, maybe win back some of what you taken off me tonight."

Marshal Redleaf stood watching Ri-ley cross the wide, dusty roadway on a diagonal, southerly course in the direction of the solitary lighted lan-tern at the lower end of town where the livery barn and public corrals were located.

He remained out front of the saloon long enough to roll and light a smoke, take the pulse of his town, finish his quirly, and walk across the road and northward to the rooming house where he had quarters, and just before bedding down reminded himself very firmly to talk to the town blacksmith first thing in the morning.

II

Enos Orcutt was at the café counter having an early breakfast when Marshal Redleaf walked in, nodded at other diners, and sat down beside the town blacksmith. They exchanged greetings before Redleaf ordered breakfast and turned to say: "Enos, I heard you were shipping out some freight."

The bull-built man, about ten years older than Marshal Redleaf, turned as he nodded his head. "Yeah. Made up ten pair of tires for the stage company on an order from somewhere up in Montana. Why?"

"Is Les Riley going to haul them?"

"Part way. Over as far as rail's end and the steam train will take them north." The blacksmith's gaze hardened a little. "What's your interest?"

"When are you figuring on sending them on their way?"

Orcutt reached for his cup, half drained it, put it slowly aside, and straightened back off the counter. "Once more, Chet . . . why? What business is it of yours?"

"I need Riley for a few days. That coach that wobbled into town yesterday. . . ."

Orcutt nodded. "The one with the warped axle and burned-out hub?"

"Yeah. It was robbed up there where the driver and his helper were removing the wheel. Four thousand dollars in greenbacks coming down here to Rodney Manion's store."

The blacksmith sat like stone for several seconds. "I heard about the wheel. In fact, I even went up there to see if anything could be done to salvage the axle. No one told me about a robbery."

Marshal Redleaf went back to his earlier topic. "I need Les as a deputy, Enos. Do you have to ship those tires right away?"

Orcutt leaned on the counter again, eyeing his half-finished meal. "No, not right away. We had some slack time so we made up the whole order. It isn't due to be sent north for another ten days." The blacksmith turned his head. "Four thousand dollars? Without no gun guard?"

Redleaf sighed. "Yes."

"What d'you need Riley for?"

"I'm going up where they raided the coach, try to find tracks, and go from there. Les is a good man to have along. He's ridden with me before a couple of times."

Enos wagged his shaggy head of graying hair. "Four thousand dollars?"

Redleaf smiled. "Can you tell him you'll be another week putting the tires together for shipping?"

"Yeah. I told him it'd be a few more days. Maybe by today. Yeah, I can tell him that. How did they get the money?"

Redleaf patiently explained, then leaned forward to eat breakfast while the blacksmith sat down again, had another cup of black java, and finally arose, cuffed Redleaf roughly on the shoulder, and departed.

When Enos Orcutt got down to his shop, the big, brawny younger man who was learning the trade from him finished tying his mule-hide shoeing apron and jutted his jaw toward the roadway. "Riley was just here. He went over yonder but he'll be back. He's sort of anxious to load up and haul out."

Orcutt stepped back to scan the roadway but it was empty in the direction of the barn and corrals. He watched his apprentice finish with the apron, then said: "Walt, we've got to go over those tires again." At the look he got from the big, younger man, Orcutt offered what he hoped would be a convincing explanation. "There were some soft spots. I didn't notice them until yesterday. Overheated iron. We've got to make damned sure that's fixed or we'll never get paid. It shouldn't take more'n another couple, three days. We'll sandwich it in between our other work."

Walt leaned down to plug horseshoe nails in the slits on the outer edge of his apron below the knees. "Sandwich it in when?" he asked grumpily. "We've got work lyin' around here that should've been finished last week."

The bear-like older man strolled to the front opening of his sooty shop and gazed northward, in the direction of the jailhouse. His attention was pulled away by someone calling his name from the middle of the road. Orcutt fidgeted as he watched Lester Riley's approach.

The freighter smiled as he came up and said: "I've been going over harness and running gear."

Orcutt reddened, told his lie, saw the disappointment settle across the freighter's countenance, and that made him feel more ashamed of himself than he'd felt in years.

Riley finally said: "Another week?"

Orcutt nodded. "Sorry, Les, but soft steel in wagon tires won't last one day's run. Walt and I'll go over them as quick as we can. I'll hunt you up when everything is ready."

Riley nodded, turned northward, passed several small business establishments including the café, passed Manion's General Store, and turned in at the pool hall just south of the saloon. Orcutt stood a long time gazing at the front of the General Store. $4,000? What in hell would Rod Manion want with $4,000, which was more money than Enos made all year?

Walt called, Orcutt went back down inside the shop, and plucked his apron off a wall peg, ready for the day's work.

On the opposite side of the road, Marshal Redleaf was finishing his first coffee and smoke for the day when he saw Les Riley shuffle into the pool hall. He killed his smoke, dumped the empty cup into a bucket of greasy water behind the wood stove, picked up his hat, and went across the road.

Les was not shooting pool because,

excluding the old man who owned the place and who did not shoot pool, there were no other customers.

When the town marshal walked in, the old man nodded at him. Like most older people in the territory whose experiences with Indians had left them anything but well disposed even toward part-blood Indians, the old man did not smile. He never smiled at Marshal Redleaf.

Les Riley was crafting a brown-paper cigarette. He glanced briefly upward, went back to finish his handiwork, light up, and say: "Good morning, Chet."

Redleaf smiled as he returned the greeting. The old man had been waiting for someone to dig out two bits for the use of a table. It did not appear the one-third Indian lawman and the freighter were going to do this soon, so he dug out a ragged newspaper and sat down to read it.

Chet asked about the load his friend was to haul out, and Riley told him the story of poor steel and more delay. Redleaf was sympathetic, and said: "I can pay a dollar a day, which ought to help defray the feed bill down yonder."

Les inhaled, exhaled, studied the lawman for a long moment, then said: "The last time I rode with you an idiot shot a horse out from under me."

Redleaf continued to smile amiably. "Those horses will eat a lot of hay between now and next week, Les. All I want to do is go up there and see what I can find. Whoever rode off with Manion's money sure as hell isn't sitting up there waiting to be caught. A dollar a day?"

Riley blew smoke, shook his head, and wordlessly followed the town marshal across the road and southward in the direction of the livery barn.

The liveryman was a balding individual with a droopy big nose that resembled an oversize strawberry and was nearly as red. As he saddled two horses, he addressed the town marshal. "Heard somethin' it's hard to believe. That crippled stage that limped into town yestiddy was raided of a box full of money comin' here for Rod Manion. Ten thousand dollars I was told."

For the first time today Les Riley smiled as they led the horses out of the runway before mounting. On the way up through town he dryly said: "Sure would be nice if a man could increase his money the way it's done in rumors, wouldn't it . . . or were you lying to me?"

"Four thousand is what Manion told me."

"He could be lying."

"Why?"

"I don't know. I'm about out of the makings. You got any?"

Redleaf passed over his Durham sack and papers. They rode a full mile warming out the horses before easing over into a lope. It was a splendid late springtime day with air so clear they could see mammoth firs atop a jagged mountain ridge thirty miles distant.

There had been traffic since the day before. There were saddle horse imprints, wheel marks, now and then cloven tracks where deer or perhaps wapiti had crossed the road.

Riley had a question as they were approaching rugged, forested land where low foothills began. "How did they happen to rob that particular stage?"

Chet was squinting ahead as he replied. "I told you . . . there was no retainer in that fore wheel."

Riley pondered that until the quirly was warming his fingers. He smashed it out on the saddle horn. "Are you telling me someone deliberately left that leather out so's the coach would have to stop up ahead?"

"Nope. Not exactly. What I think is that the leather was deliberately left out so's the hub and axle would burn, like they did, and whoever left out that leather had a friend, maybe

36

two or three friends, trailing the coach until it stopped, then they sneaked down, got the box, and that was that."

Riley scowled at his companion's profile. "Getting this out of you is like pulling teeth. How did they know Manion's money was in that box?"

Redleaf did not know. "It only happened yesterday."

Riley was not satisfied with that so he said: "Someone had to know Manion was going to have his money on that particular stage. And someone at the corral yard had to know which coach to leave a grease retainer out of . . . Chet?"

"What?"

"Manion or his clerk knew the money was coming. Someone across the road knew how to cripple exactly the right stage. What the hell are we doing up here in the trees and rocks? There's at least one man at the corral yard who can answer those questions."

Redleaf was reining toward the east-side burn and did not speak again until he had dismounted to tie his animal. When the freighter had done the same, Redleaf pointed to scuffed dust where there were no pine or fir needles, and his companion started backtracking the sign. As he was doing this, he asked a question: "Did you talk to that cranky old goat who manages the stage company in Mandan?"

Redleaf was on the far side of the tracks, also watching them, as he replied: "Nope. Didn't go near him."

Riley stopped in his tracks. "Why

not?"

"Because I don't think it could have been one of his yardmen, Les. That coach was not going north from Mandan, it was coming from up north down to Mandan."

Riley was silent for a while, then began tracking again because Redleaf was already moving northeastward into the timber. The second time they halted was where horse droppings indicated at least three horses had been tethered among the big trees for perhaps several hours, and that made Les Riley roll his eyes because it meant that whoever had been trailing the coach until it stopped had not only taken off the money box, but had not fled in haste. They had lingered in this place for several hours.

"No reason to run," Redleaf said.

"A crippled stagecoach couldn't cover ten or eleven miles in short of a couple of hours."

They found the smashed box hidden in a little ravine with pine limbs piled atop it. They found it by following the tracks of men who had walked back and forth many times to drag the pine limbs.

The address painted in black was Manion's store in Mandan. There was one more word on the smashed box in black paint. *Drygoods.*

They flung off the pine limbs, saw bruises in the wood where a steel instrument had been used to pry boards loose, to break some of them, and to knock one side of the box awry. Here, the tracks were harder to define because of needles. They finished examining the box and backtracked to the area where there were fewer needles, more rocks and dust. Here it was possible to trace outlines without difficulty.

Redleaf was experienced at reading sign. So was his friend. But the ideas that ultimately firmed up in Les Riley's mind baffled him less than they troubled him. From the beginning of the raiders' trail one thing had been obvious. The thieves had not been wearing boots; they had been wearing moccasins.

Riley hunkered across from the town marshal saying nothing. He had seen all he had to see so he eased his shoulders against a rough-barked pine tree and waited.

Redleaf quartered through the area, returned eventually where his companion was resting, sank to one knee, and said: "It doesn't make sense."

Riley cocked a quizzical eye. "What doesn't?"

"Moccasins not boots."

Riley spoke flatly. "I've heard of hold-outs ever since I got into the freighting business. I've met folks who've seen 'em slipping around in the timber or watching roadway traffic. The Army didn't corral them all." Riley pointed to the ground. "There's your proof, Chet."

Redleaf got comfortable, tipped back his hat, and squinted southward where a midday heat haze was firming up to make the world in the direction of Mandan undulate like an ocean of grass.

"Les," he eventually said, "it doesn't make sense. In the first place, if it was hold-outs, how in hell could they have known about Manion's money?"

"They didn't know, Chet. They just trailed a stagecoach until it was off by itself and crippled, then they snuck ahead and. . . ."

"Naw. Les, hold-outs don't shoe their horses. You saw the shod-horse marks back where the horses were tied. Hold-outs that I've heard about steal a lot of things . . . guns, horses, cattle, dresses and pants off clotheslines . . . but not money. Where they live in hidden places deep in the mountains, they've got less use for paper money than they have for anything." Marshal Redleaf stood up to dust off. "When you was in school do you remember reading about the Boston Tea Party?"

Riley remembered. "Yeah. A bunch of men dumped some tea off an

English ship into the water."

Redleaf nodded. "Yeah. Indians! You remember that? They were settlers dressed to look like Indians." He stopped beside the tracks and pointed. "Everything we saw up here was different from anything Indians do, Les. Except for those moccasin marks." Redleaf started toward their tethered horses, still speaking. "Those settlers who dumped the English tea wanted the Indians to get blamed. So do these sons-of-bitches."

III

On the ride back the marshal sifted through ideas that didn't fit as well as a few that did. He knew what folks would say in town the minute they heard about moccasin tracks. Instead

44

of brooding over that he had roof tops in sight by the time he rationalized that into something that could be helpful.

If enough people became angry over Indians raiding the stagecoach, it should — at least he hoped it would — distract them from what really happened back there. If there was enough denunciation about Indian raiders, whoever in Mandan knew what had happened up there, how, and why it had happened, would probably feel safe.

He did not say anything about this. Not even after dusk when he and Les Riley had handed back the livery horses and went over to the café for supper, and later strolled to the jailhouse for some coffee and relaxation.

It was Riley who finally put things

into perspective; he did not mention the moccasin tracks. He said: "All right. That grease leather was taken off up north, maybe at Berksville, the place where most local stages lie over, then head back, but that don't explain how someone knew the money was in that box."

Redleaf handed his friend a cup of hot coffee, returned to his chair, and sank down. "You said they trailed the coach and raided it when it was forced to stop. You said they didn't know there was any money. They just got lucky."

Riley shifted in his chair, eyed the steaming coffee that was too hot to drink, and muttered his reply: "Yeah. Well, that's how it seemed up there."

"But not down here?"

"No. I don't believe that much in

coincidences." Riley leaned to put the cup aside, then settled back, legs pushed out. "It's got to be someone right here in Mandan, Chet. Manion's clerk. Maybe that cranky old man who manages the stage company. Maybe Manion himself shot off his mouth."

Redleaf was almost smiling as he regarded his troubled friend. "You're pretty good at backtracking," he said. "Let's backtrack right now. Let's go talk to Manion. Why did he need that money? Did he owe someone four thousand dollars? Maybe he was going to invest it in something. Someone he was doing business with one way or another knew he'd need four thousand dollars. If Manion will tell us that, we can hunt him down."

Les Riley shot up out of his chair.

"That's what I been trying to figure out."

As the lawman rose, he smiled in the direction of the roadside door as he said: "You get good ideas, Les."

The Manion residence was on the south side of a dusty side road on the east side of town. It was one of the few painted residences in Mandan. Even from a distance it had a look of prosperity. The little picket fence out front was painted; the gate did not sag. Beyond, there was a wooden walkway to the elevated porch. The house had two stories and there was a light in the parlor as well as in one second-floor room as Riley and Redleaf approached the front door.

Light temporarily blinded both men when a graying, tall, and statuesque woman opened the door. She did not know Les Riley, so she bobbed her head in his direction, but she knew Marshal Redleaf and greeted him with a smile as she moved aside for them to enter.

The interior of the house smelled wonderfully of recent cooking. There was a log fire at one end of the overly furnished parlor where the men felt heat. Redleaf introduced Riley to Rod Manion's wife. She acknowledged his presence with another quick, brusque little nod.

Redleaf asked about her husband. She told him she had sent for the doctor from up at Berksville and that he should arrive tomorrow. When the lawman asked if they could talk to her husband, the tall woman hung fire, eyeing them both, before curtly nodding and turning to lead the way.

Rodney Manion's upstairs bedroom smelled of some variety of dried and crushed flowers that had been simmered in hot water.

The storekeeper recognized his callers. He was propped up in the bed, pale, drawn, and unable to remain still; he either tapped the counterpane with his fingers, or jumped his eyes around the room, across the ceiling, down to the faces of his visitors, or at his wife, who stood primly by, hands firmly clasped over her stomach.

Riley unobtrusively sat on a chair that was near the farthest reach of an overhead lamp. Marshal Redleaf stood at bedside, smiling downward. "You're looking pretty good," he told the man in bed, and got a waspish retort.

"You aren't going to find those

thieves in my bedroom, Chet."

Redleaf grinned as though it had been a joke. "Rod, we found the box, some tracks, but nothing else. What we'd like from you is some information."

The storekeeper's brows dropped a notch. "What information? Chet, they're putting miles between Mandan and them right this minute."

Again Marshal Redleaf ignored the waspishness. "Why did you need that four thousand dollars, Rod?"

Manion's pale blue eyes stopped moving and remained fixed on Redleaf's face. "For business," he explained. "For increasing the inventory. For having money on hand to cash voucher checks for stockmen."

Redleaf watched the older man closely. "Right away, this week?

Couldn't you have waited until the stage company could put a gun guard on the coach?"

Manion's gaze sprang from Redleaf to Les Riley and back. "I was running low on cash," he answered, deliberately not meeting his wife's stare from half in shadows. "In business a man has to keep a supply of cash on hand. If I'd waited until the stage company put a guard on, I might have had to wait until next year."

"You could have hired one, Rod."

Manion snorted. "It's not up to me to provide protection for the stage company."

Redleaf guided the conversation back where he'd wanted it earlier. "You didn't have any other reason for withdrawing that money from your

Denver account and having it sent down here disguised as drygoods?"

Manion steadied his gaze with an effort. "Just for business purposes. If you operated a general store, you'd know what I mean."

Redleaf twisted to trade glances with the freighter. Both the storekeeper and his wife noticed this. The tall woman spoke sharply to Marshal Redleaf. "Do you doubt his word, Chet?"

Redleaf smiled at her, and evaded a direct reply. "What I'm trying to figure out is who knew he had sent for that money. Someone besides your husband knew it was coming." Redleaf turned back to face the man in the bed. "I'll do my damnedest to get it back for you, Rod, but I can't do it alone. Who knew you had sent for the money?"

Manion stared at the far wall a few inches over Marshal Redleaf's left shoulder. It became so quiet in the room it was possible to hear a large old clock ticking down in the parlor.

"Howard knew," the storekeeper finally said. "My wife knew."

"No one else?"

The ticking clock reached the ears of everyone in the upstairs bedroom before Manion spoke again. "A man staying down at the rooming house named Henry Nye. He knew."

Redleaf's dark brows shot up. He knew everyone in Mandan and its environs. He had never heard that name before. "Who is he, Rod? How did he happen to know the money was on its way down here?"

Manion glanced at his wife as

though for support. She remained flintily erect and expressionless. Manion brought his attention back to Marshal Redleaf. "He's a mining engineer. Chet, I can't tell you more than that."

Riley arose, hat in hand. He'd felt the intensity of the looks Manion had shot at him. He said — "I'll wait downstairs." — and left the room. Behind him the storekeeper's wife also departed. She caught Riley on the ground floor to ask if he had accompanied Marshal Redleaf north to the site of the theft, and, when Riley told her that he had, she looked intently at him as she asked what they had found up there.

Riley regarded the statuesque woman thoughtfully, and decided now would be a good time to start circulating the moccasin story. He had no way of knowing what the tall woman's reaction would be, but he found out right after he said: "Yes'm. We found the box where they'd tried to hide it. We found where their horses stood and we found moccasin tracks. Plenty of them."

The tall woman straightened to her full height, clasped both hands across the front of her apron, and fixed Riley with a fiercely triumphant look. "I knew it! I told Rodney he was losing his mind if he did business with that man!"

She spun around and went stamping back up the stairs and passed Chet Redleaf midway without even looking at him. He paused to watch her disappear beyond the door of her husband's room, shrugged, and continued down until Les Riley said: "For what it's worth, she asked me what we found up yonder, and, when I said we'd found moccasin tracks, she looked like she was going to explode and went charging back upstairs."

They left the house, turned west beyond the neat little picket fence, continued until they were on Mandan's main thoroughfare, then turned south again toward the rooming house near the lower end of town.

Not a word passed between them until they were approaching the darkened porch of the rooming house, then Les Riley brushed the marshal's arm and spoke in a lowered tone of voice.

"You believe in hunches? I've got one now. We're going to be halfway home when we walk in on this Nye feller."

The rooming house had a set of rules nailed to the roadway door. Chet knew them by heart. He had lived here for five years. The front door was locked tight sharply at 10:00 P.M. and would not be unlocked until 5:00 the following morning. Roomers were to remove boots before going to bed. Tobacco chewers would find a spittoon in each room. If they missed it, they would be charged extra for cleaning up.

As they pushed inside, a crippled old man turned to scowl from his elevated position on a chair. He had been jockeying a clean glass chimney on the hall lamp. When he recognized Redleaf, the scowl did not leave. He was gingerly getting down from the chair as he said: "You know rule number seven. No overnight guests unless paid for in advance."

The marshal ignored this to ask where a man named Henry Nye was staying. The old man jerked his head. "Room Six. Opposite your room." The old man's scowl changed slightly. "No trouble in the house, Chet. What's he wanted for? Any bounty on him?"

They brushed past. Redleaf rattled the door with a knotty fist. They had to wait a couple of minutes after a deep, growling voice told them to be patient.

When the door finally opened, Henry Nye had lighted a lamp, which was behind him. Redleaf and Riley stood like statues. Henry Nye was not only an Indian; he was one of the biggest Indians either of them had ever seen. He was easily six feet and four or five inches tall and he was built appropriately for that height. Riley guessed he had to be at least two hundred and fifty pounds.

He returned their stares, motioned them into the room with an arm like an oak, stuffed shirt tails into his britches, and eyed Chet's badge. He said: "I hope it's important, Marshal. Being awakened from a sound sleep never helped my disposition much." He pointed to a pair of chairs. "Sit down." He went to a coat hanging from a peg, produced two thick cigars, and offered them to his callers. They both declined, so the big man lighted one stogie and tossed the other atop a dresser, dropped down on his bed, and scratched his head.

His hair was coarse, straight, and very black. He wore it short. His features were neither thick nor fine, but somewhere between. He was, in fact, a handsome man, and certainly impressive. His hair was graying at the temples. He glanced briefly at Riley, put his attention upon Chet Redleaf, and removed his cigar to speak.

"What can I do for you, Marshal?"

Chet cleared his throat. Henry Nye would have been a shock in broad daylight. In the smoky lamp glow he looked big enough to wear a saddle. Chet explained about the stolen money, how it had been stolen, and ended up by saying he and Les had just come from a visit with Rodney Manion and that Manion had mentioned Nye as one of four people who had known the $4,000 was coming to Mandan.

The big man chewed his cigar for a moment, black eyes fixed on Marshal Redleaf. One thing was becoming clear about Henry Nye; he was not a man who could be hurried. He removed the cigar again and spoke while examining the length of its ash.

"Marshal, I'm a mining engineer with a diploma and a degree from a Massachusetts University. I'm not a stage robber. I knew the money was coming because Mister Manion is investing in a location I discovered while vacationing in the mountains northeast of Mandan two years ago." Nye plugged the big cigar back between large white teeth and continued to stare at Marshal Redleaf. "I heard about the theft from Mister

Manion yesterday. That's about all I can tell you."

Chet had a question. "Who did you tell that you and Rod Manion were going into the mining business together?"

"No one. Not a soul." The black eyes were fixed unblinkingly on Redleaf's face.

Les Riley sighed noisily and looked at his friend. "So much for your idea, Chet."

But the lawman was not finished. "When did you arrive in town, Mister Nye?"

"Four days ago. I came up on the northbound coach from Daggett. I've been on the road for five weeks. I had to go back East to arrange for mining machinery. It should arrive within the next ten days . . . Marshal?"

"Yes."

"Did you go over the place where the box disappeared?"

"Yes, and we found the box, among other things."

"Then why aren't you out with a posse? The longer you wait, the farther off they'll be."

Chet arose, hooked both thumbs in his shell belt, and said: "Because chasing them would most likely take us all over hell, and there's someone here in Mandan who can give me some answers, if I can find him."

The big man spread hands the size of hams. "I'm not your man."

IV

It was late when Chet brewed coffee atop his office stove. Mandan was quiet, at least until some night-prowling varmint stirred up the town dogs. Les slouched in a chair squinting in the direction of the roadside door as Marshal Redleaf went to his chair, saying: "What was that you said . . . if we found Nye, we'd be halfway home?"

Riley yawned behind a thick hand before answering. "It's a start, ain't it? Moccasin marks up yonder and one hell of a big Indian who talks like a schoolteacher. All we got to do is connect the moccasin sign with the big Indian."

Marshal Redleaf inhaled deeply of the coffee's aroma. "We started out to find out why Rod needed all that money. Well, we found out, and you know what? We're just as far from sorting things out as before. Maybe more so. Now we've got Henry Nye to add to our list."

When the coffee boiled, Redleaf drew off two cups, passed one to his friend, and returned to the table with the other cup. "It's late," he stated, and tested the coffee, which was too hot.

Riley agreed. "Must be after ten o'clock."

"You want to go with me while I roust Manion's clerk out of his blankets?"

Riley's raised cup stopped in midair. "Right now? What's wrong with waiting until morning?"

Redleaf smiled bleakly. "Nothing. I just feel like doing it now. I never liked Howard Ballew."

Riley sipped coffee in silence. When the cup was empty, he rose tiredly, hitched at his britches, re-set his hat, and ran a palm along the slant of his jaw to make a raspy sound.

They left the jailhouse lamp lighted, emerged into an empty, dark roadway between outbursts of barking by local dogs, and turned north as far as an empty site between two buildings, crossed the Westside alley, and angled among other empty places to reach a small house where old logs had been sheathed over in front with planed boards.

Manion's clerk lived alone. When he had first arrived in town three or four years earlier, there had been the usual speculation. By now people accepted him, so most of the gossip had died out. But Ballew had never contributed to it earlier, and still did not. He was a close-mouthed, lean six-footer with a lipless wide mouth, curly brown hair, a prominent Adam's apple, who looked to be in his middle thirties and, while he was co-operative at the store, kept to himself when not working there.

Chet Redleaf's reason for disliking the tall man was difficult to define. He had tried to analyze it a couple of times and gave it up. One thing he knew was that Howard Ballew did not like Indians. Not even Indians who were mostly white. But that recognizable subtlety had not actually annoyed Chet. He'd been encountering it since late childhood, and had shrugged it off because it was not really a common thing among people he had known.

As he raised his fist to rattle the door, Les Riley brushed his arm and jerked his head. Mystified, Chet followed his friend down off the porch and around behind the house where there was a pole corral and a three-sided shed. Inside the shed was a tall bay horse eating calmly from a raised manger. He turned a curious stare at the two men climbing into the corral but went right on chewing.

Les chummed his way up close, put a hand on the bay's neck, and motioned for the lawman to do the same. The bay horse was sweaty. He had been ridden not very long ago.

They groped in darkness for the saddle and blanket. The blanket was also sweaty on the hair side. The saddle, draped high by one stirrup, still felt warm on the sheep-pelted skirts.

Les dryly said: "He's not going to

be asleep after all."

They returned to the front of the house. As they were approaching the door, Chet lowered his head softly to ask a question: "How did you know from here that horse had been ridden?"

Riley held up a hand for absolute silence. The sound of the animal masticating reached them through the utterly silent dark stillness.

Chet raised his hand to rattle the door, and this time there was no interruption.

First, a lamp guttered to brightness, then the sound of someone stamping into their boots was audible; after that there was a quiet interval before a tall, lean, and sinewy man opened the door with a six-gun in his fist. When he recognized Redleaf, he lowered the gun, stepped aside for his visitors to enter, and without a word or a smile closed the door while gesturing them toward chairs.

The parlor was not much larger than an ordinary bedroom and it was chilly. As Chet moved toward a chair, he managed to brush the iron wood stove. It was cold.

The tall man turned up his parlor lamp to spread light, and, as he was doing this, the marshal asked if he had any ideas about Manion's money and what had happened to it. The tall man finished fiddling with the lamp before shaking his head as he sat down. "The only thing I know is what Mister Manion told me when he came back from the stage company's office where they'd told him his box had been stole off the rig while it was stopped."

"He was pretty upset, Howard?"

The store clerk almost smiled. "Upset? Yeah. He was about to have a screamin' fit. He broke into a sweat, mumbled, and flung his arms around. Finally he went home. I heard he was flat out in bed with the doctor comin' from up at Berksville."

The clerk leaned back as though he was deriving some satisfaction from all this. "You know Mister Manion as well as I do, Marshal. There's nothin' on this earth that'll set him off like losin' money. Nothing at all. All he thinks about is makin' money."

Ballew paused to gaze at his visitors. He had a lantern-jawed, long face. He looked from Chet to Les Riley and back. "You got something on your mind?" he asked.

Redleaf smiled. "Howard, why did Mister Manion tell you he was sending out for that money?"

It was a trap, and for once one of Chet's traps was properly sprung. The lanky man answered without hesitation. "He said we was running short on operating capital to cash vouchers with and such like."

"Who did you tell he was sending for the money?"

Ballew's long face acquired a rock-hard cast; he glared at the lawman. "No one. Is that what you're doin' out here tonight, tryin' to involve me with his money gettin' stolen?"

Marshal Redleaf's reply was calm. "What we're trying to do is find anything at all that'll help us figure out what happened. Did Mister Manion mention any business propositions or investments, anything like that?"

Ballew's mood was no longer co-operative. "He wouldn't discuss things like that with me. I just clerk in his store. We aren't partners or anything like that."

The visit ended shortly after this, and, as Riley and Redleaf were carefully picking their way across refuse-littered back lots in the direction of the lighted jailhouse, Les said: "Well, he knew the money had been sent for. You got that much out of him, and so far he's the only one outside of Manion, his wife, and that big Indian who admitted knowing that."

Redleaf opened the jailhouse door for his companion to precede him as he replied. "That's just about everybody we've talked to. Are you getting tired, Les?"

Riley reddened as he entered the warm, lighted office, dropped down in the chair he'd vacated an hour earlier, and scowled at Redleaf. "Yeah, I'm tired, and I'm going down to my wagon to bed down right after you tell me why you didn't ask Ballew how come his horse was sweaty so late at night."

Chet draped his hat from a wall rack of antlers before seating himself. "Because he's the only suspect we got so far that's been out of town late at night."

Riley looked perplexed. He seemed about to speak when the marshal beat him to it.

"We wouldn't be likely to pick up his tracks from all the other tracks around town, so I guess we've got to keep watch over him. Not while he's at the store, but afterward. In case he makes another ride late at night. And he rode that horse fairly hard. I'd say a man who rides hard late at night heading away from home, then returns the same way, isn't pleasure riding."

Les Riley eyed the coffee pot atop the wood stove, but, when he rose, he walked past to the roadside door and spoke with one hand on the latch. "How about that big Indian?"

Chet leaned back, hands behind his head. "If we had a telegraph in town, I'd send out some enquiries about him. Since we don't, I guess we'll have to keep an eye on him, too." The marshal rose to approach his friend with a smile. "You sleep in tomorrow. I'm going to have another talk with Rod Manion. I think I know why he didn't want to talk about his four thousand dollars."

Riley nodded. "Yeah. Because of his wife. She went up those stairs like the devil after a crippled saint when I mentioned moccasins. Good night."

Redleaf closed the door after the freighter, returned to his table, rolled and lit a quirly, and sat in thought for a half hour before locking up from outside and heading for his quarters at the rooming house.

The roadway door was locked. He knew better than to rattle it because the old man either slept like the dead or pretended to. He went along the west side of the old building, hoisted his window, and climbed inside. For precisely this reason the window was never locked.

He had the lamp lighted and was coiling his shell belt and holstered Colt when someone rapped lightly on his door. He draped his hat from a nail in the wall, crossed over, and opened the door.

Henry Nye filled the opening, fully clothed and smelling strongly of cigar smoke. Redleaf jerked his head, closed the door, and pointed to the only chair in his room. Nye eyed it warily, decided not to put it to the test, and went over to lean against the window sill as he said: "You've been busy tonight, Marshal. I looked all over town for you. I knew you'd be back directly because the lamp was lighted in your office and the stove hadn't been dampered down."

Chet sank down on the edge of his bed. "Yeah, we've been busy. What can I do for you?"

The big man's very dark eyes shone in the lamplight. "Tell me about those moccasin tracks you found up where the coach stopped."

Redleaf thoughtfully considered the large man. "Not much to tell, Mister Nye. They were all over the place, but mostly in dusty places where a little kid could have seen them."

"Hold-outs, Marshal?"

Chet gently shook his head. "I'd guess they weren't Indians at all but white men wearing moccasins to make it look like the robbery was done by Indians."

"But you do have hold-outs in those northward mountains, Marshal. I'm not much of a redskin. I was born and raised in a religious compound in upstate New York. But there's always something in the remembering blood, I think. When I was prospecting up there a couple of years ago, I got the feeling that I was being watched, so I began sneaking around to do some watching of my own."

"And you saw Indians?"

"Yes. Several times. They never approached very close. My guess was that I was in an area they hunted over, or maybe camped in. I pretended I didn't see them. Marshal, maybe you're right. Maybe it was whites wearing moccasins, but I know for a fact you have hold-outs back in the mountains who wear moccasins."

Chet began rolling a smoke. The large man watched him in silence. When he had lighted up, he smiled at the big man. "I could use some help, Mister Nye. It might be in your interest to lend me a hand. I'd like to get Mister Manion's money back. But mostly, I'd like to know who stole it."

Nye eyed Redleaf warily. "Well, I'd like to see you recover the money, Marshal, but I'm a stranger to this country, and I'm not a manhunter, so I don't know what I can do."

Chet kept his smile up. "I'll arrange for a saddle animal for you and some supplies. If you'd ride back up where you have that mining claim and sort of settle in like you're going to stay for a while and, when those Indians scout you up again, see if you can maybe catch one, or let them catch you."

Nye's black brows climbed. "Why?"

"Because, Mister Nye, I've got a

feeling that if those hold-outs scouted you up, they scout up other folks who either pass through their mountains or camp up there."

Henry Nye's face cleared. He was thoughtful for a moment before saying: "Marshal, what kind of Indians are up there?"

Chet laughed. "Darned if I know. Wild ones I guess."

Nye missed the humor. "I can speak a little Mohawk. Darned little. And they sure as hell aren't woodlands people, are they?"

Chet leaned to stub out his smoke in a smashed-flat tin can that served as an ashtray. "They could be Crows, or Southern Utes, or maybe a mixed band." He straightened back. "As sure as I'm sitting here, there'll be some who speak English."

Nye seemed to accept that, but he mentioned something else. "Tell me, Marshal, are there stories of them killing travelers or hunters up there?"

Chet shook his head. "Not that I've heard. My guess is that they'd do just about anything to avoid something like that, because, if they did it, their mountains would be crawling with soldiers and posse men." Chet could not resist so he also said: "Of course, there's always got to be a first time. Do you own a six-gun?"

Henry Nye continued to lean on the sill for a long silent moment before pushing upright as he answered: "Yes, a six-gun and a Derringer, but I'm not a very good shot . . . maybe if I took something up to give them. . . ."

That was an excellent idea. "Three

things they'll be short of, Mister Nye, are salt, sugar, and coffee. You'll do it?"

Nye smiled. It was the first time Redleaf had seen him look other than solemn or annoyed. "Yes, but suppose we keep this between the two of us. If there are men down here in Mandan involved with that robbery, I'd just as soon they didn't know I was going into the mountains to find Indians who might have seen them, might be able to identify them as the thieves."

Chet agreed to meet Nye down at the livery barn an hour before sunrise to see him on his way. After the large man closed the door and crossed the hall to his own quarters, Chet sat slumped on the edge of his bed, wagging his head because now he dared not sleep, or, as tired as he was, he'd never awaken in time to help the big man get organized for his trip to the mountains.

V

Riley killed almost a full hour at breakfast. He also sat out front of the jailhouse in morning chill for a long time, and finally went stamping down to the rooming house.

Chet was returning from the wash house, an old gray towel draped over his shoulder when the freighter entered from out front. Les said: "Have you seen Manion yet?"

Redleaf hadn't. He had not gone to bed until shortly before sunrise, which was shortly after he'd seen Henry Nye heading north in the darkness.

They entered Redleaf's room where Les leaned indolently, waiting for the lawman to finish dressing, buckle his weapon belt into place, and reach for his hat.

Out front Les said: "If you're going to see Manion, I'll make coffee at the jailhouse."

As Redleaf passed the café's steamy window, he was tempted to turn in. Instead, he walked the full distance to the storekeeper's residence and was admitted by Manion's wife, who greeted him but did not smile as she did so.

Upstairs she remained primly erect while Redleaf approached the bed. Rod Manion needed a shave. He had been fed; the tray was still on a small table at the bedside. He looked enquiringly at the town marshal.

It had been Redleaf's hope that Mrs. Manion would not remain in the room. She was clearly not going to leave, so Chet placed his old hat carefully aside, drew a chair close to the bed, and said: "Rod, tell me about the mine."

Manion's tall wife unexpectedly emitted a loud snort of derision and stamped out of the room, slamming the door after herself.

Redleaf listened to angry footfalls going down the stairs before speaking again. "I talked to Henry Nye."

Manion seemed to loosen beneath his blankets. To emphasize his relief at being alone with Chet, he also heaved a great sigh before beginning to speak.

"Henry came to the store a while

back for supplies. We got to talking. He offered me a half interest for five thousand dollars. He drew up papers and I gave him one thousand out of my office safe." Manion pointed toward a small table with a marble top. "In the top drawer, Chet."

Redleaf went to the table, picked up a small but fairly heavy little doeskin pouch, and returned to the bedside with it. Manion said: "Open it."

The pouch contained four gold nuggets. The smallest one was slightly larger than a bean. The largest nugget was about the size of Chet's thumbnail. Manion handed him a glass half full of water. Chet dropped them into the water one at a time. They sank like lead. He leaned back on the chair. "They're gold all right," he said. "The next question is . . . how do you know Nye is as genuine as his nuggets?"

Manion smiled slightly. "I've been gambling on my ability to judge folks for a lot of years. In my business, where you got to extend credit, you learn to make judgments about people. Henry's genuine."

Chet gazed at the water glass, thinking that if Nye wasn't genuine, if Manion had misjudged this time, Chet had presented the big Indian with the means to leave the country. He said: "I hope you're right, Rod. Now I've got one more question. Does your clerk have friends out in the country somewhere . . . maybe a girl he's sparking?"

Manion slowly wagged his head on the pillow. "He don't spark girls. At least I've never known him to in the three or so years he's worked for me."

"How about friends?"

Manion's pale eyes were fixed on the lawman. "You know Howard. He puts in long days at the store, maybe has a drink at the saloon. Otherwise he don't mix much."

Chet was leaning to arise when Manion stopped him. "Howard . . . ? You think Howard . . . . ?"

"He knew the money was coming, Rod."

"So did Henry Nye. So did my wife. Maybe others knew, too."

Chet smiled and stood up without mentioning Ballew's night ride. "Yeah, and that's my problem. Rod, I'll find your money, if it can be done. Get back on your feet." He gave the older man a rough slap on the shoulder, and departed.

Manion's tall wife was waiting for him in the parlor. As he came down the stairs, she said: "I told him from the beginning he was losing his mind, that Henry Nye was another educated redskin who'd learned white ways and like all of 'em was out to use what he knew about white folks to get even with them."

Chet's temper was stirring, but, as he put on his hat, he smiled at her while going to the door. "I sure hope you're wrong," he said, and let himself out.

By the time he reached the jailhouse, his anger had died. Les had hot coffee. Chet told him what Manion had said. When he told him about the nuggets, Les's brows climbed like twin caterpillars. "If something like that got out, there'd be folks up there with picks and shovels scouring every hillside and meadow."

Chet rolled a smoke. He was hungry but this would dampen the feeling for a while. After lighting up, he told Les about his pact with Henry Nye, and the freighter stared back without saying a word for a long while. Not until Marshal Redleaf had drawn himself a second cup of coffee to take back to the table with him.

"And suppose that big Indian just keeps on riding? Suppose he's in cahoots with the men who robbed the coach?"

"We'll be skunked," replied Marshal Redleaf. "But I'll bet my wages for a year he'll do what neither you nor I could do. He looks like an Indian. I don't. Not enough like one to go up there and try chumming with them."

Les slumped in his chair, sipping coffee. Into the silence that settled between them the blacksmith's big, muscular apprentice appeared from out front to tell Riley the blacksmith wanted him to know the wagon tires would be ready to ship north by the middle of the following week.

After the younger man had departed, Les gazed dispassionately at Marshal Redleaf. "Whatever gets done had better get done before next week."

Chet nodded. He was thinking ahead. "I'll watch Howard Ballew tonight. You can do it tomorrow night."

Riley looked doubtful. "Not if you were up all last night. All we need is for you to fall asleep tonight, if Ballew rides out again. That'd set us back another few days and I'm freighting north next week come hell or high water. You bed down and I'll spy on Ballew."

Chet left Riley out front, walking southward, while he headed for the café, ravenous as a bitch wolf. Jack Hudson, the burly barman, was at the counter when Redleaf sat down. Hudson looked around, nodded, and went back to his meal until after the café man had come and gone, then he put down his tools and said: "The whip who brought in the morning stage from Berksville came in for an early jolt this morning before he had to take another coach southward. I guess they're short of drivers. He told me there was some kind of ruckus up in Berksville a few days back.

Something about a corral yard drunk gettin' troublesome. The marshal up there flung him in one of his cells and by God the hostler had one thousand dollars on him, which is pretty good for someone who don't make more'n, at the very most, thirty dollars a month."

Hudson continued to look steadily at Marshal Redleaf after he had finished speaking. The café man brought Chet's platter and departed. Hudson nudged the lawman. "You don't suppose that yardman got part of Rod Manion's money, do you?"

Redleaf picked up his knife and fork as he answered. "If he did, Jack, he sure as hell got an awful big share of it."

Hudson left the café. Chet finished eating and walked out into the sunshine, looking southward. There was no one in front of the livery barn. He struck out in that direction with an idea firming up in his mind that had occurred to him at the café counter.

Riley was out back with his wagon. When Chet came up behind him, he was already stating his reason for being there. He told Les what Hudson had told him, and added a little more. "If you'll take the stage north and find out all you can from that yardman in the Berksville jailhouse, I'll spy on Ballew tonight."

Les tipped down his hat to keep sun glare from his eyes and gazed at the town marshal. "On one condition," he eventually said. "That you go down to your room right now and get some sleep. Ballew will close the store about six o'clock. If you sleep between now and then, I'll go north, and, if that's the yardman who removed the grease retainer from the coach that got robbed, I'll get it out of him one way or another."

Chet nodded. "See you in the morning." He left Riley gazing after him, went directly to his quarters, shed his boots, gun belt, and hat, dropped onto the bed, and within five minutes was asleep.

When he awakened, early evening was settling. In the roadway two arguing men were using language most of Mandan's residents, particularly the female segment, did not approve of. Chet rolled up into a sitting position, yanked on his boots, stood up to buckle his gun belt into place, grabbed his hat, and went down the dingy hallway to the roadway where he paused to clear his pipes, rub his eyes, and stare at a small crowd of onlookers who were watching two head-to-head big freight wagons whose angry drivers were demanding that each other back clear and make way.

The road was blocked. There was buggy and light wagon traffic behind both wagons. Horsemen could go around the big rigs, as could people on foot, but nothing else could pass.

Redleaf walked out into the road-way, down the near side of the clos-est wagon, which had entered town from the north, stepped to the hub from the ground, used improvised hand holds to climb higher. The onlookers were motionless. The op-posite teamster was no longer shout-ing. The man whose wagon the lawman was climbing on, baffled at the abrupt silence, leaned to look down his near side.

Redleaf's face came even with the teamster's face. The teamster was a swarthy, beard-stubbled man with too-long hair and soiled clothing. He saw the badge.

Chet reached, got a handful of shirting, and heaved backward with all his weight. The freighter squawked, let go of his lines, and reached frantically for something that would break his fall. When he hit the ground on his back, some rough men among the onlookers laughed. Chet came back down to the hub, jumped to the ground, leaned over the stunned teamster to disarm him, flung his six-gun toward the crowd on the sidewalk, and started toward the other huge wagon.

This time the freighter could not be taken by surprise. He saw the town marshal coming for him and slammed off his binders, leaned back on the lines, and yelled for his eight large mules to move backward. They obeyed. It was to the teamster's credit that he could back his hitch without crimping the front wheels. His wagon was half empty, which made it easier to be backed.

Redleaf stopped to watch, turned slowly toward the other teamster who was struggling to catch his breath, hoisted the man to his feet, and said: "You get up there and do the same. And don't you ever come down Main Street again with that big wagon. You use one of the back alleys. If you don't, the next time I catch you out here, I'll impound your outfit, auction off the mules, and raffle off your wagon. Now get up there."

It required fifteen minutes for the big wagons to squeeze as closely as they could to one sidewalk or the other, and inch past one another. The drivers did not even look at each other as they did this.

Marshal Redleaf stood on the plank walk in front of the saloon, watching. When the road was clear, he went down to the café for an early supper. The counter was empty when the café man came along, drying both hands on a soiled towel and smiling. He was a taciturn man but he had observed the interlude in the road. He said: "That was a good lick, Marshal."

Chet acted as though he had not

heard. "Steak, spuds, coffee, and pie if you've got it. What time is it?"

"Half hour before six."

A pair of townsmen entered the café, both bachelors. One was the blacksmith's helper, the other a yardman from the stage company's corral yard. They exchanged nods with the marshal and went farther down the counter.

When Redleaf had finished and stood up to pay, he asked the yardman if the late-day stage going north had left town. It had.

Outside, the fading day had a faintly smoky cast to it as though it might rain, but as nearly as Redleaf could tell there were no clouds.

He crossed to the jailhouse, pulled a chair to one of the little, barred front windows, and got comfortable.

Across the road he could see customers inside the General Store being
waited on.

He had one interruption and took
advantage of it. The elfin, small,
bowlegged man who owned the livery
barn poked his head in to say he'd
seen the tussle in the roadway and to
compliment Redleaf on the way he'd
handled it. Chet asked the liveryman
to saddle a good horse and leave it in
a stall. At the quizzical stare he got
about this, the marshal simply said:
"I might want to use him, and I
might not. But if I've got to, I'd like
to have him rigged out and ready."

The bowlegged older man winked
conspiratorially, closed the door, and
went hiking briskly southward.

Chet drew off a cup of java, rolled
a smoke to go with it, and got com-

fortable at the window again. Failing daylight had sheathed Mandan in soft tan. It had not appeared to get any darker for the last hour or so, nor would it. At this time of year the days were longer, and, even when dusk eventually arrived, it settled with infinite slowness.

Chet had finished his coffee, put out his quirly, and was sitting in near darkness behind the thick walls of his jailhouse by the time he saw Manion's lanky clerk bolt the front door of the General Store from the inside, blow down the mantles of the three lamps that lighted the store, and shed his apron and sleeve protectors while standing at the roadway window, looking up and down the roadway.

Chet sighed, got to his feet, went through the rear storeroom behind his office, and out into the alleyway. It was lighter out there than it had been in the jailhouse.

He walked to the north intersection of the alley with a side road and waited for Ballew to enter the saloon for his usual nightcap.

He did not enter the saloon when he emerged from a dogtrot but stopped on the plank walk in front of the General Store to glance around before striking out in the direction of his little house on the west side of town.

VI

The lingering dusk was more of an obstacle than an ally. Redleaf could not follow the store clerk across the open area between the alley and his residence without being seen. He watched Ballew stride toward his residence while using the alley and its flanking buildings to conceal himself, but Ballew looked neither right nor left. Chet got the impression that the lanky man had something on his mind. He hoped it might be supper and that Ballew would take his time about rustling it up and eating it. It was time for the lawman to make a decision, but he waited to make it until he saw Ballew climb through corral stringers behind his house to fork a bait of hay to the big brown horse.

Horses were usually fed twice a day, once in the morning, once in the evening. It was also customary to feed a horse that was to be ridden an hour or two before he was saddled and bridled. Chet had to gamble this was Ballew's reason for feeding the bay before feeding himself. He turned back down the alley in the direction of the livery barn in a swift walk. There was no one around as he went up the runway, looking for a saddled horse in a stall. What he found was a large, powerfully built dark mare with a blazed face and a couple of white socks.

He led her out, snugged up the cinch, checked the bridle, and, because he did not know her, he led her out back and turned her twice before cheeking her to get astride. She acted thoroughly tractable. He walked her up the alley. She was one of those strong animals with lots of bottom that telegraphed all this to the man on her back through the seat of his britches. He swung off a few yards shy of the northward intersection, trailed the reins, and moved ahead until he had a clear view in the gradually increasing evening of Ballew's distant house.

There was a light burning. Chet's tension slackened off a little. He rolled and lit a smoke, growled at the big mare when she tried to reach over someone's old wooden fence to bite heads off some flowers, and decided that, rather than run the risk of being discovered, he would remain in the alley until Ballew rode away. Otherwise, he could have scouted around through the increasing darkness to be closer. The main risks of doing this included the fact that his mare might nicker at the smell of the bay horse, or the bay horse might alert

Ballew that a rider was out there somewhere, by nickering first. The light abruptly flickered out.

Redleaf still stood in front of the big mare. He was not certain but he thought he saw a silhouette move from the rear of the house toward the corral. Finally he left the alley with the mare close on his heels, and continued to walk until he could vaguely make out the house, the corral, and the horse shed. He saw nothing but he heard the sounds of a man rigging out an animal, turned to swing across leather, and hold the mare on short reins in case she decided to nicker. She didn't, but she clearly knew the bay horse was ahead in the warm night; she stood like a statue, head raised, ears forward.

Redleaf hoped she wasn't horsing,

otherwise she would certainly fidget and eventually trumpet to the gelding she could scent but not see. If she had done those things, Redleaf would have had something hair-raising to say to the liveryman when he got back to town. *If* he got back to town.

The big mare was strongly curious about the scents up ahead but she neither offered to nicker nor to fidget. Chet sighed. He was not a man who rode mares. He wouldn't have been astride this one if he'd had a choice. The sound of a ridden horse heading northward eventually told the town marshal all he had to know. He waited until the sounds were almost indistinguishable, then allowed the big mare to follow.

After about a mile of trailing the

bay, the big mare seemed to understand what her rider was doing. It may have been coincidence, but, when Ballew suddenly halted up ahead, the mare stopped dead still. When Ballew rode on, the mare moved out. She kept the distance without pressure from the reins. Chet leaned to pat her neck. She would not change his opinion of mares but she encouraged his admiration of her as an individual mare.

Full darkness made it possible for the marshal to worry less about being seen, but he still had to be alert in case the store clerk did as he had done earlier, stop to listen. They were about three miles north of town when Ballew eased over into a lope. Because a loping horse made more noise than a walking horse, Chet could keep track of his prey without trying to keep up with him. He knew the country they were passing through. It was flat to rolling. The closer they got to the uplands, the more uneven it became. He knew the territory up ahead, too, but that did not help any in trying to guess where the store clerk was going.

When Ballew hauled back down to a walk, Chet eased ahead a little so as not to lose the sound of the big bay horse. He was speculating about Ballew's destination, not about why he was out here, when the big mare missed a lead as her head came up and swung slightly to her left. Chet could see nothing out there, but the mare had either heard or smelled something, so he eased her back a little.

Ballew turned west in front of a solitary old twisted pine tree, which was evidently a landmark he had been seeking in the darkness. Chet halted, listened, and also moved westerly when Ballew's sound was very faint. He thought he had hung back too far and squeezed the big mare to close up the distance a little. She obeyed but there was no horse sound up ahead. There was no sound at all.

Chet acknowledged a shrill little silent alarm in his head, stopped, and swung to the ground with one hand raised to the mare's cheek piece in case she nickered. If Ballew was still moving, he was crossing sand, or perhaps something as sound absorbent like deep dust, because Chet could not hear a thing.

The moon was coming. Farther out high rims were bathed in an eerie glow. Chet started walking with the big mare. There was concealment up there, but northward where some uneven low hills appeared, not out where he was leading the mare. He had lost Howard Ballew.

He tried to recall ever having seen ancient lava dust up here, something anyway that absorbed sound, and could not for the life of him remember anything but hard ground, tall grass, rolling countryside, and very few trees. The mare plodded until something brought her head up very abruptly as she leaned back slightly on the reins. Chet halted, but whatever had caught her attention was invisible to him, and soundless.

He waited a long while before moving out again, and he was now beginning to feel uneasy. Ballew had not been swallowed up by the night, nor had Chet encountered anything like sand or deep dust, but it only belatedly occurred to him that the store clerk was no longer riding. It was the big mare that brought this realization home when she finally sucked down a deep breath and raised her head.

Chet's fingers closed down like a vice before she could whinny. She tried to toss the hand off, failed, and, when he finally eased up enough for her to breathe, she was too occupied doing that to try to nicker. Ballew was up ahead. Someone was, anyway, and whoever it might be was being silent and perhaps wary. Chet turned back to find something to tie the mare to and had gone no more than a hundred yards when a silhouette seemed to rise up out of the earth directly in his path. It had to be a fairly solid silhouette because it cocked a Winchester.

Chet yanked the mare to a halt, hoped the silhouette could not see him do it, and eased his right hand slowly toward his hip holster to tug free the tie-down thong.

A sharp voice said: "Both hands over your head!"

Chet obeyed. The silhouette did not move for a full minute, then it slowly approached, carbine held belt buckle high in both the man's hands. When they were close enough to see each other's features, the armed man said: "Well, well, well. He was right. It was you that got the saddled mare from the livery barn. Marshal, use your left

116

hand to lift out the six-gun and drop it. But if you think you can beat a trigger pull, you just go right ahead and try it."

Chet, left-handed, lifted out his weapon and let it fall. He was trying very hard to place the coarse-featured face of the man fifteen feet away. His effort was interrupted by a voice he had heard often speak from behind: "Who is he, Cuff?"

"The marshal from Mandan. You cover him, and I'll see if he's got any hide-outs."

The rearward man was silent as he took several forward steps and halted to await the results of his companion's search. Chet gave up on the man who had caught him. If he'd seen him before, he could not remember it. But the man behind him was Howard Ballew. As the stranger stepped back, eased down the hammer of his Winchester, and grounded it, Howard Ballew walked around where he could see Redleaf's face. He was holding an uncocked Colt in his right fist. He gave his head a little wag before speaking. "Too bad, Marshal. Turn west and walk ahead of me. Stay on the left side of the big mare. I'll tell you when to halt."

Chet had said nothing to this point and did not say anything now as he turned and started walking. He was angry with himself for having been captured so easily. Without question the man who had captured him had already been out there, watching Ballew's back trail. That being the case, Chet had no one to blame for being caught but himself. He should have suspected Ballew was riding to a rendezvous. If he hadn't been concentrating so hard on keeping track of the store clerk in the darkness, he probably would have realized both he and Ballew were inevitably going to meet someone out here.

"Halt," Ballew said, and raised his voice a little. "Fred, it's the town marshal."

Another man Chet did not remember having seen before came up the gentle slope of a swale, carbine slung carelessly over his shoulder. He was thick, weathered, and bearded. He eyed Redleaf in silence until Ballew ordered the marshal to proceed down the slope, then the bearded man fell in beside him, studied Redleaf's profile as they walked, and finally said: " 'Breed Indian. You're the lawman down at Mandan?"

Chet nodded, eyeing the scattered horse equipment down where there was a camp.

The bearded man smiled. "I thought it was supposed to work the other way . . . white skins gettin' caught by redskins."

Chet turned, scanned the bearded man's face, then replied: "Naw. If that was true, there wouldn't be any white skins. It worked the other way. White skins always slipping up on redskins."

The bearded man nudged Redleaf toward some upended saddles and told him to sit down with his hands in his lap. He did not seem very fierce or hostile, maybe because he did not have to seem that way. But the other stranger and Howard Ballew were different. They sank down on the ground, eyeing their prisoner, clearly troubled by this unexpected situation.

The bearded man who had been called Fred ignored Redleaf as he rummaged for a plug of chewing tobacco and bit off a cud of it. He addressed the store clerk. "Well, Howard . . . ?"

Ballew did not look at the bearded man when he spoke. "I stopped and listened. He didn't make a sound an' it was too dark to skyline him while he was moving."

Fred turned to expectorate, turned back, and addressed the other man Redleaf did not know. "Cuff . . . ?"

"I was fixin' to come to camp behind Howard. I thought I heard somethin' so I got flat down an' here he come, leading that big mare. He wasn't no more surprised than I was."

Fred sprayed amber again. "The point is . . . what do we do with him?"

Ballew sounded vindictive when he replied to that. He probably was embarrassed about not having known he was being trailed. "Nothing we can do but shoot him. We can't take any chances. An' we don't have all night. It's a long ride back to town to get the money out of the store safe an' go over and burn old Manion's feet until he tells us where he's got his savings hid."

Chet stared at the clerk. "What money?" he blurted out. "Why would he have four thousand dollars sent down here if he already had money?"

Ballew raised sulphurous eyes to the marshal. "Because he wouldn't touch his savings to save his damned soul. I happen to know he's got a lot of money cached somewhere in town. And there's the money I've taken in at the store since he's been sick at home. It's not a whole lot but it hadn't ought to be left behind."

Chet stared at Ballew. "Then why didn't you bring it with you tonight?"

Fred chuckled. "Howard, he ain't dumb."

Ballew ignored that to snarl his reply to Redleaf: "Because Miz Manion comes in an' counts the receipts. Not every day but I could never tell when she might do it. If that damned money and I was gone, she'd tell her husband, and sure as hell we'd never find his savings."

The man who had caught Chet fidgeted. He was holding his carbine across his lap. "You don't have to explain nothin' to this son-of-a-bitch, Howard, and we're wastin' time. It's gettin' late. We got a lot of ridin' to do before we get this done with. Howard, you want to shoot him or do you want me to do it?"

Fred spoke up: "Maybe we'd ought to take him along, sort of like life insurance."

The man called Cuff snorted about that. "Fred, for Christ's sake, we're goin' to have enough to do without watching him, too."

Fred caved in. "Have it your way, Cuff. Howard . . . ?"

Ballew leaned to push up off the ground. When he was upright, he said: "On your feet, Redleaf. We're goin' for a walk."

VII

As Cuff and Fred watched Ballew herd the town marshal up the easterly slope, a very distant, faint pewter light appeared. Evidently the moon had arisen sometime before and had been obscured by clouds. Now, where the ghostly paleness appeared, visibility was not helped much but the heavens took on an unusual luminosity. Redleaf did not notice. Neither did the man walking behind him a couple of yards. When Ballew thought they had walked far enough, he halted and started to give an order when somewhere behind him in the direction of the camp a horse loudly trumpeted.

Instinct flashed a warning to both the prisoner and his executioner.

Horses whinnied like that at the scent of other horses, riders, something that aroused their curiosity without frightening them. Howard Ballew twisted to look back. Redleaf was too far ahead to rush him. He cocked his head to listen as he said: "Riders. They're coming from the north."

Ballew faced forward. "Get flat down an', if you make a noise, I'll blow your head off. There's only supposed to be one."

Redleaf moved a little closer to the store clerk before lying down. To keep up the tension he said: "They're angling toward your camp. You hear them?"

Ballew hissed at him: "How can I with you spouting off every couple of minutes? Shut up!"

Chet held his upper body off the

ground with his elbows, peering northward. He whispered — "Sounds like maybe four or five of them." — closing both hands around piles of loose soil, dust, and tiny rocks.

Ballew also raised up. "I don't hear anything." He turned with a deep scowl and Redleaf raised up, hurled the fistfuls of dirt, and sprang ahead. Ballew instinctively raised both hands as his eyes filled with dirt. He made a sound in his throat as instinct told him to get back, get clear. It was too late. Redleaf hit Ballew with his shoulder, bowling him over. The store clerk would have had his hands full even without being blinded and in pain from his eyes. Redleaf hit him twice, the first time as Ballew was rolling his head. That blow grazed upward through Ballew's hair at the temple. The second strike landed squarely against Ballew's jaw below the ear. He arched suddenly, and just as suddenly went limp.

Chet took the six-gun, dropped it into his own holster, stood up, listening, and was reassured by the lack of sounds from the direction of the camp, and sank down to check on the unconscious store clerk.

He straddled Howard Ballew, gazing westward. In a soft voice he said — "I owe you, old mare." — stood up, flexed his knuckles, and eyed the pewter sky. Enough time had elapsed so he tipped Ballew's six-gun upward and fired one shot. Echoes chased one another in all directions.

He shucked the empty casing, plugged in a fresh load, and walked northward until he felt safe, then turned westerly, and finally halted on the gentle slope of the same shallow arroyo where Ballew's friends were waiting. The odds were not in Redleaf's favor except for one factor. Fred and Cuff had heard one gunshot out where Ballew had marched his captive to be shot. They would expect Ballew to return to camp soon. Chet started southward on the lip of the arroyo until he could hear a man's intermittent grumbling. He went back a few yards from the edge of the arroyo, still moving parallel to it. When the grumbling became distinct, desultory conversation between Fred and Cuff, Redleaf turned westward in a silent stalk.

The burly, bearded man called Fred spoke in a manner that was evidently characteristic of him: "You're like

Howard, you're forever expectin' the sky to fall on you. We still got plenty of time. Here, have a drink."

The less resonant, faster-paced voice of Cuff replied: "An' suppose someone finds his body out here?"

"Have a drink, damn it. Nobody's goin' to find . . . Cuff, who would have a reason to be out here? Just us an' Paul, an', if he hasn't come by now, he ain't coming. Hey! Don't drink it all!"

Redleaf belly-crawled to the lip of the shallow place, put his hat aside, raised his head, and had better visibility than he'd had before the moon had located that thin place in the overcast. He could see Fred facing him and Cuff with his back to the slope.

Without a sound he eased Howard

Ballew's six-gun ahead, rested the butt on the palm of his left hand, and waited for that desultory talk to resume before cocking the weapon. It was not a very long wait. Cuff finally pushed up off the saddle he'd been leaning on. "What the hell is taking him so long? Fred, if we waste another damned hour, we might as well forget goin' down there tonight. It'll be daylight before we even reach Mandan."

Fred remained unperturbed. "All right. Then we'll ride down there tomorrow night. One damned day ain't going to make much difference. Cuff, you been worryin' ever since we left Berksville."

"Yeah, I been worrying. I told you six months ago Jim Brooks was a damned drunk. Now they got him in jail up there, and, believe me, Fred, he'll tell 'em everything. He's got jelly for backbone."

Fred remained unruffled. "If he tells them, what can they do about it? We're out here in the middle of nowhere, it's too dark for 'em to track us, even if they knew it was us that left the tracks."

Cuff shook his head. "They don't have to track us. All they got to do is send word down to Mandan about Brooks takin' out that grease leather, an' sure as hell he'll tell them he done it, if they throw him up against the wall a few times. You know what'll happen then? The law an' most likely half the town'll be waitin' down there for us."

Fred made a scornful snort. "You're puttin' the horse behind the cart. In the first place the law of Mandan is out yonder with a slug in him. In the second place, even if Brooks tells them everything an' they send the word down to Mandan that him and us, Howard, and the blond feller who works for that Mandan blacksmith, got Manion's money, all they will know is that we left town. That's all. We left town in the night an' could be riding in any direction."

Redleaf spoke into the silence that followed Fred's argument. His voice carried perfectly. He neither raised it nor sounded very menacing, but, as he was speaking, he watched the pale men in the swale very closely: "Put your hands straight out in front of you."

Cuff, already tightly wound, started up off the ground. Fred's surprise was just as complete but his temperament was different. He sat perfectly still, gazing up the slope in the direction of Redleaf's voice. He was not sure whose voice it was from up there, but he knew it was not the voice of Howard Ballew.

Fred put both hands in front, arms rigid from the shoulders. Cuff, half bent around toward the slope, had a twisted face with bared teeth showing.

Redleaf spoke again. "You better do it or you'll never leave this place standing up. Face forward, you bastard. Put your arms out in front like your friend is doing!"

Fred muttered something indistinguishable without taking his eyes off the top-out where Chet was prone. Cuff gradually eased down, faced ahead, and raised his arms.

"The guns," Chet said. "One-handed and toss them backward."

They disarmed themselves as he had ordered. As Fred did this, he asked a question. "Where's Howard?"

"Back yonder with a bad headache and a sore jaw. Stand up. Both of you. Now walk toward the sound of my voice."

Cuff was angrily silent but Fred spoke as the pair started eastward up the gentle slope. "Marshal, a man workin' for wages just keeps on pluggin' and hopin' and one day he's old and ailin' and he's still workin' for wages."

Chet rolled to his feet as the men came closer, gestured with Ballew's handgun for them to walk out where he had left their companion, and told

Fred to keep quiet, but Fred was a wily individual and kept up his harmless ramblings until it dawned on Redleaf that what Fred was doing was letting Howard Ballew know they were coming.

He approached the burly, bearded man from behind, swung the pistol barrel in a short, fierce arc, stepped back so as not to be struck by the falling body, and looked straight at Cuff, whose mouth was hanging slack. "Get down there and tie him," Chet said. "Use his belts and cinch them up tight."

Cuff knelt, touched the unconscious man, and raised a hand. "You cracked his skull . . . he's bleeding."

"Tie him and keep your mouth closed."

It did not take long. Cuff pushed

up to his feet with most of that earlier defiance gone. When Chet gestured for him to start walking again, he obeyed without a word or any hesitation.

Ballew was still lying where he'd been knocked unconscious, but his body was beginning to make small, spasmodic jerks as consciousness slowly returned. Chet told Cuff to sit down with his hands in front. He rolled the store clerk onto his back, hoisted him, and propped him against a knee. Ballew groaned, raised a feeble hand to explore his jaw, which was turning purple and was also swelling. He looked into the marshal's face from a distance of about twelve inches, let his head tip forward slightly as he turned toward Cuff.

Redleaf stepped away from them a few feet and sank to one knee with Ballew's six-gun hanging loosely. Ballew finally said: "Where's Fred?"

Cuff told him, and glared. "How in the hell did you make a mess out of somethin' as simple as shootin' an unarmed man, Howard?"

Ballew did not respond. Chet answered for him: "He heard riders out yonder when that mare whinnied."

Cuff's brows dropped. "Howard . . . what's wrong with you? You spent all your life in stores? That damned mare is comin' into heat. She'd whinny at her own shadow."

Ballew still would not raise his head. Chet went over them both for hide-outs, did not find any, and got comfortable in the cooling night. He would have worried about other riders coming to this place if he hadn't heard Cuff and Fred discussing the other men involved in stealing Manion's money, and who had met out here with the store clerk to be led back to town to get even more of the store owner's wealth. Only two of them were not out here. Jim Brooks, the corral yard hostler up at Berksville, and big Walt Prentice, the town blacksmith's helper. And maybe a third man, someone named Paul.

He did not worry about Brooks, who was probably still in the Berksville jail, trying to explain that thousand dollars he'd been carrying when he'd been locked up. He did not particularly worry about Enos Orcutt's helper down in Mandan. If Prentice had not arrived at the rendezvous by now, it was highly unlikely that he would. Redleaf's surprise at learning there were two men in his town who were involved in stealing Rod Manion's $4,000 did not last long.

Ballew asked if anyone had brought the bottle of whiskey from the camp. Cuff would not even look at him, so Chet answered: "No. When we saddle up to head for Mandan, maybe we can find it for you."

Ballew slumped. Cuff cast a sidelong glance at Redleaf and asked if he could get a chew from his shirt pocket. Redleaf nodded, cocked Ballew's six-gun, aimed it at Cuff's middle, and did not lower the hammer or let the gun hang slackly until Cuff had his cud in place behind his left cheek. He looked across at Redleaf, spat, and said: "How long we goin' to sit here?"

"Until there's enough daylight for me to keep an eye on all of you. Then we'll saddle up and leave."

"It's gettin' cold."

Chet nodded agreement about that. "Sure is. What do you want me to do, build a fire?"

Cuff turned aside to spray tobacco juice again, faced forward looking menacingly at Marshal Redleaf without speaking.

The chill increased as dawn hung just beyond the farthest curve of the world. Someone behind them in the direction of the empty camp called out gruffly: "Where the hell is everybody?"

Chet smiled a little. Even with an oversize headache that Fred could not avoid having right at this moment, he was still garrulous.

Chet jutted his jaw at Cuff. "Tell him."

One more spray of tobacco juice, then Cuff called out: "We're settin' over here like sage chickens waitin' for dawn."

"Who is? Was that you, Cuff?"

"Yeah, it was me. I'm over here. So is Howard, an' the town marshal is settin' here with us, holdin' a gun."

"What the hell's he waitin' for?"

"Dawn. Some daylight to see by. I just told you that. Are them belts still tight, Fred?"

"They're tight. Too tight, an' my head feels like there's a kickin' mule inside it tryin' to bust out."

Cuff looked at Redleaf, expecting him to react some way to Fred's dilemma. Chet sat there without moving or making a sound. Occasionally he would glance eastward where the sun would appear before too long. He was cold and hungry and had been wondering about Les up in Berksville, and big Henry Nye in the mountains looking for hold-outs. If he could get his prisoners back to Mandan and locked in the cells down there, maybe he could send word to Berksville for Riley to return, but there was no way he could reach Henry Nye. He hadn't even been sure where Nye would be in the mountains. Trying to find him would be impossible.

Ballew suddenly swung his arms to keep warm. There was a streak of sickly gray spreading along the eastern world, the cold was as bad as it would be for the rest of the day. Fred called profanely that his legs and arms were stiff and sore.

Chet finally rose, gestured for his prisoners to walk westward, and paced along behind them until they reached the burly, bearded man whose old hat had been punched down over his ears by the force of the blow that had knocked him senseless. Cuff knelt to free his friend without looking at Chet for instructions, nor looking at him afterward as he helped Fred stand up, and steadied him. Fred lifted his hat with both hands. He had a thick mane of iron-gray hair. Even so, there was a slight matting of blood-encrusted hair where the gun barrel had come down. His eyes were bloodshot.

None of them looked presentable as they trudged back down the gentle slope where their horses were already moving along, cropping grass.

VIII

If the big mare was horsing, she did not do it as hard as most mares did. Even so Chet kept her away from the other horses as the little group started riding southeastward in the cold early morning. By daylight they all looked dirty, haggard, unshaved, and sunken-eyed. Two of them, Ballew and the man called Fred, had not been helped much by the whiskey Chet had found at the camp. Ballew was morose, but Fred, possibly with a thicker skull to go with his garrulous, rather practical disposition, slouched along like a man who was resigned to his fate. Once he said:

145

"Marshal, you don't get paid enough for the hours you got to put in."

Redleaf responded tartly: "I suppose you do."

Fred did not look back where Redleaf was bringing up the rear as he replied: "Yeah, I think so. We miss a little sleep now 'n' then an' once in a while got to postpone a meal, but we make as much in two months as you make all year. I know because I was a town marshal once."

Chet's interest was piqued. "Where?"

"Over in Idaho. North end of the Snake River. . . . Marshal, suppose you could pick up as much from us as you'll get as a lawman for the next year?"

Chet looped his reins and went to work over a cigarette. "I wouldn't take it," he said matter-of-factly. "I don't like missing meals and losing sleep. Fred, tell me about the blacksmith's helper down in Mandan."

The bearded, burly outlaw raised his hat gingerly to explore his injury before replying: "Nothin' to tell."

"He was the one who saw me leave town. How did he get word to you and Cuff?"

"Heliograph mirror from upstairs at the rooming house. Marshal, you're lettin' a real fine opportunity get away from you."

Redleaf smiled. "Is that a fact? You boys got four thousand dollars from that crippled stage an' there are five of you. That's not a hell of a lot of money per man for all the ridin' and worryin' you had to go through."

Cuff spoke for the first time since

they'd been astride. "Amen. That's the gospel truth."

But Fred ignored that to say: "That was for openers, Marshal. We was to get maybe as much again, maybe more, from the storekeeper's cache down at his house. And on the way out of the territory we'd pick up a little more from stages and what not."

Howard Ballew put a venomous look upon Fred. "You always did have a tongue hinged in the middle that flapped at both ends. Shut up!"

Fred was not particularly intimidated. He eyed Ballew briefly before addressing him. "If I was in your boots, I don't think I'd criticize other folks. You led him right to our camp, and fell for a schoolboy trick when you walked out a ways with him."

Ballew ignored the other man. In

fact, he did not speak again, even after they could see roof tops in the distance, but Cuff did. He'd been evaluating his situation. "I got a question for you, Marshal. What would it take for you to look the other way for fifteen minutes before we reach town?"

Redleaf gazed dispassionately at the speaker. "Whatever it is, you don't have it."

Fred, who had already asked a similar question, eyed Cuff sardonically. But he did not speak.

Chet led his prisoners down the west side alley with late-day shadows beginning to emerge, left the horses with a big-eyed hostler, and marched his prisoners to the jailhouse. On the way people stared, some gathered out front of the saloon and General Store to speculate aloud. Down in front of the blacksmith's shop no one emerged to stare, but, as Redleaf followed his prisoners into the jailhouse, he knew that his arrival back in town with prisoners would reach the shop before very long, as it would spread elsewhere through town.

He had the prisoners empty their pockets atop his table, took them into the cell room, and locked them into cells. He was returning to the office when Fred called after him. "How are you goin' to prove anything?"

Chet did not answer. He slammed and barred the cell-room door, left the office with a thrusting stride, heading toward the lower end of town. People watched but prudently made no attempt to accost him.

Enos Orcutt and his helper were

out back under a sooty overhang struggling profanely to pry a large rear wheel off the axle of a jacked-up dump wagon. Neither man looked up as the marshal came out and stood under the ancient overhang, watching.

That livery barn day man who had cared for the horses came rushing into the shop, eyes wide. He got halfway through before he saw Marshal Redleaf, standing there. Evidently his purpose in arriving had been to give Orcutt the latest news — that Redleaf had returned to town with some prisoners — but, when he saw the marshal, he did an abrupt about-face and walked as swiftly back out of the shop as he had walked into it.

Orcutt and his big, powerful apprentice finally got the wheel jarred loose. They braced on both sides of it to work it free. As it began moving, Enos looked over the shoulder of his helper and said: "Damned cowmen never put grease on nothing until it's too late, then they complain that wagon makers don't make 'em like they used to."

Walt Prentice looked around, saw Redleaf in the shade, nodded, and braced for the final rocking to get the wheel off. When it came, its weight nearly caused both the men holding it to fall.

Prentice rolled it to an upright, and carefully leaned it there, while his employer walked over to Marshal Redleaf, wiping both hands on a dirty old rag. He said: "You been out of town. Folks have been speculating.

Did you find anything?"

Redleaf did not take his eyes off the big apprentice who was shaking his head as he examined a rusted, badly pitted wagon axle. "Yeah, I found something, Enos."

Walt Prentice looked around, showing interest. Redleaf jutted his chin. "Him."

Neither the blacksmith nor his helper moved. They stared until Chet rested his right hand upon the handle of his six-gun, then Enos Orcutt turned with a bewildered expression to stare at his helper. Prentice ignored Orcutt. He began drying both palms down the outside-seam of his trousers.

Chet said: "Take off the apron, Walt. I want to see what you got beneath it."

The big muscular man stared at Redleaf. "What are you talkin' about?" he demanded.

Redleaf repeated it. "Take off the apron!"

Prentice pulled down a big breath and used both hands to untie his shoeing apron as he let his breath out.

Chet's intuition was right. He raised his left arm to push the blacksmith away, gripped his gun with the other hand, and, as the shoeing apron fell to the ground, Prentice pushed out both hands, palms up. He was not wearing a gun belt beneath the apron.

Chet gave another order. "Pull up your pants' legs."

Prentice obeyed until the tops of his boots showed. There was no hide-out weapon. As he was straightening up, he smiled. "What else you got in mind, Marshal? We got a lot of work to do around here."

Redleaf jerked his head, still gripping the gun handle. "Walk up the middle of the shop to the roadway. Cross over out there and walk up to the jailhouse."

Enos Orcutt's bewilderment had not diminished but his patience had. "What the hell are you doing?" he demanded of the lawman. "He's been right here with me all day. Yestiddy, too."

Chet replied without taking his eyes off Walt Prentice. "He didn't have to be anywhere else, Enos. There were five men involved in stealing Manion's box off that crippled stage. Your helper here was in it up to his hocks."

Orcutt's bewilderment deepened. He looked from one of them to the other, then made a fluttery gesture with his hands. "Chet, are you sure you know what you're doing?"

"Dead sure, Enos. Prentice, like I said, walk up through to the roadway."

As the powerfully built large man started moving, Chet lifted out his six-gun. Prentice passed within ten feet of him. He kept on walking. Inside, where daylight rarely reached, the shop was black with layers of soot. There were anvils bolted to massive old oak rounds. There was a forge where the metal canopy was warped from heat and greasy black from many fires. There were tools along the south wall held in place by loops in a long leather hanger. There were other tools where someone had left them.

As Chet started up through behind Orcutt's apprentice, the big man passed close to an anvil where tools had been left. Chet was watching closely, but the big man knew this would be the case. As he started past the anvil, he did not look around or downward, but he listed a little, and before Orcutt or Redleaf saw a change, Prentice had picked up a pair of tongs used for pulling metal from the forge, turned on the balls of his feet, and hurled the tongs as hard as he could.

Redleaf instinctively ducked. Orcutt, who was behind him, was slower. The tongs were wide open when they hit him in the chest.

Prentice hurled a pipe-handled shoeing hammer and followed this with a horseshoe nail-hole pick. The pick struck Chet in the shoulder as he was tipping his gun muzzle. There was little pain but the momentum moved his body to the right as Walt Prentice broke away in a lunging run, and emerged from the shop into the roadway as Chet fired.

The bullet punched a hole in Enos Orcutt's most cherished copper bucket. Where it exited it left a jagged place large enough for a man's fist to fit through. Neither Orcutt, who was recovering from being struck by tongs or Marshal Redleaf who was swinging his gun for one more shot before Prentice disappeared across the road into the livery barn, were concerned with the bucket. Chet went rapidly toward the roadway. Enos started after him, but stopped up near the anvil where Prentice had counter-attacked and prudently remained there. He did not have a gun.

Redleaf was in the shop doorway when a waspish explosion across the road was followed by a board on the front of the shop a foot away, bursting apart under the impact of a bullet. Deeper in the barn's runway a man's startled squawk suggested where the big apprentice blacksmith had gone. Chet looked left and right, then started over there, but kept to the right of the doorless barn opening in case someone shot at him again from inside the old building.

No one did. He got across without incident. Northward people were tumbling from buildings on both sides of the roadway to gape southward. Redleaf did not hesitate in front of the barn. He knew Prentice would be trying to get a horse to flee on. He did not believe Prentice would be foolish enough to break clear of the barn out front, so he slipped down among the old cribbed pole corrals toward the rear alley. There was noise inside the barn. Redleaf was almost to the alley when he heard a frantic voice say: "Get the hell away. I don't need no saddle."

Chet widened his steps and was at the juncture of the barn with the alley when he heard a horse rise up and come down in a hard lunge. Prentice was astride bareback. Chet settled against the north side of the barn, raised his weapon, and, when the big blacksmith's helper came charging out of the barn, Chet was ready. But Prentice did not turn right up the alley, he turned left, which was southward. Chet jumped to the center of the alley and yelled. Prentice twisted and fired twice. Chet fired once. Prentice was firing from the back of a terrified, running horse. Chet was stationary with a large target dead ahead. The big man slumped, dropped the six-gun he'd got at the barn to grip the running horse's mane with both hands, while Chet lowered his Colt and remained, wide-legged, in the middle of the alley, watching.

Several noisy townsmen came running down through the barn from up the roadway. Chet ignored them even when they burst out into the alley yelling questions at him. Prentice was down low over the horse. As distance made it difficult to see him clearly, Chet yelled up the barn runway for someone to saddle him a horse, then resumed his position, expecting Prentice to fall any moment. He did not fall.

He was getting small in the afternoon sunlight by the time Chet was handed a pair of reins, mounted without even looking at the animal beneath him, and started southward from town in a slow lope. He was half a mile along before he thought there was something familiar and looked down. He was riding the same big mare he'd ridden before. He swore. She had already been put through a hard ordeal. If Walt Prentice didn't fall to the ground up ahead, that fresher animal he was straddling would very probably draw away from the big mare as the horse race went on.

Redleaf did not push his animal. He did not particularly want to overtake Prentice; he wanted to keep him in sight until he collapsed with his mount running out from under him. But the big mare viewed things differently. She thought this was supposed to be a horse race and steadily widened her stride, eyes fixed on the other horse, the one she thought she was supposed to catch.

Chet laughed, eased back on the reins until she was down to a lope, patted her roughly on the neck, and said: "You are some critter, Mamie, or whatever your name is. When we get back, I'm going to buy you if I can. Not to ride, mind you, but just to turn you out, and, when I find a two-legged female that can match you for brains, marry her."

Far back several townsmen were coming in a flinging run, coattails flapping, hats being pulled down. Chet watched them, faced forward, and saw Walt Prentice aiming for a bosk of white oaks. He corrected the big mare, aiming in the same direction. He did not hurry. In fact, he rode steadily slower until he was down to a walk. If a man was like a wounded deer, sometimes the best thing to do was to sit patiently and just wait.

IX

Walt Prentice was off the horse among the trees. Chet could make out a fidgeting animal in speckled shadows, but he could not locate its rider. He thought that, providing the big man's gunshot wound was serious, he would be flat on the ground among the trees. He knew Prentice had dropped the six-gun he'd acquired back at the livery barn, and a reasonable assumption would be that he was now unarmed. Most of the cemeteries west of the Missouri River had occupants who had bet their lives that someone had been unarmed when they hadn't been.

He waited, and, when those flinging riders from town came sliding to a halt nearby, sprang to the ground, and rushed forward, Chet stood beside his mount with a hand raised. He knew the townsmen. One of them gestured in the direction of the bosk of trees and called loudly that they had seen the fugitive ride in there.

There were five of the excited

townsmen, all armed, all agitated. Chet told them to stay back out of the way. Not to use their weapons no matter what they thought they saw up ahead. He stood with the mare's reins draped from an arm and rolled a smoke under the scowling looks of the townsmen. After lighting up, he ignored them to kneel, facing the trees. The horse was no longer excitedly moving and there was no sighting of Enos Orcutt's apprentice. Chet smoked, eyed the sun, glanced around at the muttering townsmen, and faced forward again.

A townsman said: "What'n hell's the sense of doin' nothing? There's enough of us to surround them trees."

Chet replied without taking his eyes off the distant bosk. "He's wounded.

We're not going to do anything. It's up to him."

"You hit him?"

"Yes."

"Then he's likely dead in there an' evening's coming."

Chet stubbed out his smoke, glanced at the patiently standing big mare, and ignored the townsmen. Waning daylight cast thickening shadows angling in the direction of the trees. The waiting men were not so distant from town they could not detect the fragrance of smoke from supper fires.

A man called from in among the trees. "Redleaf, you can set there all night, I'm not coming out!"

Chet's reply was dryly spoken: "That's all right with me, Walt. In the morning we'll come in and wrap you in a blanket and haul you back stiff as a ramrod."

The townsmen were impatient. One of them departed in the direction of town, too disgusted to remain. Chet allowed the big mare to crop feed to the length of her seven-foot reins, and continued to wait.

Dusk was sifting in like faint soot when the same voice called from the trees: "Redleaf! Why me?"

"Because I've got all your friends except Brooks in my cells, and the one called Fred told me you signaled from the rooming house with a mirror when I left town. He also told me all the rest of it. Walt, I can set out here for as long as it takes. You're not going anywhere, not even after dark. We'll get completely around your trees after dark and, if you try slip-

ping away, you're going to get yourself killed. Walt, for you this is the
end of it. The others'll get supper and
a bed up off the ground tonight.
You'll get yourself shot to death. It's
not worth it."

There was no more conversation
until dusk was fully down, then Prentice called again: "You got a canteen,
Marshal?"

Chet did not but one of the townsmen had and called to Prentice:
"Yeah, there's water! There's also
some whiskey."

The blacksmith sounded tired when
he finally caved in. "All right, Marshal? I'm not armed!"

"All right. Walk out with your hands
even with your shoulders. No one'll
shoot."

"Just one arm, Marshal, the other

one's busted an' I can't raise it."

"Walk out. Leave the horse."

Every man out there watched the darkening gloom of the trees. No one moved or made a sound. It seemed to be an interminable wait, but it was actually only about ten minutes before Prentice appeared as a pale silhouette backgrounded by tree gloom. He was leaning heavily on a crooked length of deadfall wood and halted just clear of the trees until Chet reassured him, then he continued to walk.

The townsmen muttered as Chet rose from his stooping position. He growled at them to stay where they were and not to touch their weapons. He was walking toward Prentice when he said that.

The big man had blood on his shirt

and trousers. Even in poor light he looked like someone who had been butchering beef. His color was ashen, which Chet could not make out, and he was listing heavily to the side of the tree limb he was using as a support. Redleaf stopped fifteen feet distant. They eyed one another for a moment before Walt Prentice fainted. One moment he was standing there; the next moment he was lying on his face.

Chet called for the townsmen to fetch the big mare and come up where he was standing. As they were obeying, he knelt to roll the large man on to his back.

Prentice had a shattered right arm with glistening white bone ends protruding through flesh and shirt cloth. It was not just a broken arm, it was a lifelong, crippling injury, and he had tied off the flesh above the wound with a torn piece of cloth, but there had been a considerable loss of blood. Even in poor light, the townsmen lined up as solemn as pallbearers.

Chet gave orders as he examined the tourniquet, eased the lifeless-appearing lower arm inside Prentice's shirt front, and wiped blood off his hands in the grass.

"One of you fetch the horse in the trees. We'll boost him across a saddle and ride on both sides to keep him from falling off. One of you gents can ride the bareback horse."

A townsman leaned to stare as he said: "How much blood's left in him? He's soaked with it."

Chet ignored that: "Bring up a

horse!"

They had to grunt because even though there were five of them, including Marshal Redleaf, Prentice was not just heavy he was also inert.

They started back with dusk darkening toward full darkness. There was no moon but the night was warm and would probably remain that way for another couple of hours. Their progress was very slow, but, by the time they had lighted windows in sight, they had worked out a fairly efficient method of keeping the unconscious man atop a horse.

In the alley behind the livery barn they eased Prentice to the ground, and, while the townsmen were handing reins to the night hawk, Chet went searching for a blanket.

They placed Prentice on the blanket

and went awkwardly up the back alley to the rear door of the jailhouse, carried him inside where Redleaf lighted a lamp, and laid him out flat on the floor. The townsmen left, presumably making a beeline for the saloon, leaving the marshal to care for the unconscious large man whose shattered arm was becoming very swollen above the tourniquet and corpse-colored below it.

He got water, some clean rags, and washed away most of the dried blood. Enos Orcutt arrived, looked shocked at what he saw, and spoke in sepulchral tones when he said: "I'll send someone up to Berksville for the doctor. Marshal? Are you sure he's alive?"

Chet nodded as he rose, drying his hands. "He's alive. He'll lose that arm sure as hell. When he comes around, he may not want to face that, Enos. And I've got a feeling we can't wait for the Berksville doctor."

Orcutt looked horrified. "What are you talkin' about?"

"See for yourself. The lower arm's shattered with bone splinters all through it. The slug must have hit him squarely in the back of the arm. Look at it. He looks like a half-butchered sheep."

Orcutt felt for a chair and sank down, staring from the man on the floor to the town marshal. "Chet, for Christ's sake. . . ."

Redleaf hurled the bloody rag at the floor and turned on the blacksmith. "All right, Enos. You're his boss. It's up to you, but it looks to me if someone doesn't amputate that arm below the shredded part he'll never make it. Go ahead, loosen that tourniquet. See what happens. If he's got to lie here until tomorrow afternoon when a stage can get down here from Berksville, I wouldn't bet you a plugged *centavo* he'll live long."

"Marshal, cuttin' that arm off isn't going to. . . ."

"Kneel down here while I hold the lamp. Now then . . . do you see that dirt in the meat? He'll have an infection in his body by morning that'll kill him no matter what a doctor tries to do."

Redleaf hung the lamp back on its ceiling hook and leaned from the hips against his table, gazing at Orcutt's helper.

Other townsmen arrived. Chet growled at them the moment they opened the door. As they retreated after a good look at the bloody man on the floor, there were no more interruptions until those men had returned to the saloon and or to their homes around town to tell what they had seen. Then both Enos and Marshal Redleaf got a surprise.

Big Jack Hudson walked in out of the darkness without his little bar apron, but still wearing his pink sleeve garters above the elbow and his elegant brocaded vest with three cigars in each upper pocket. He closed the door, ignored Redleaf and Orcutt to stand a moment staring at the ashen man on the floor, then he crossed closer, sank to one knee, growled for someone to lower the lamp. When Redleaf complied, the big barman rolled up both sleeves and made a careful, thorough examination.

It was quiet enough inside the office to have heard a coin drop. Hudson stood up, fished forth a large handkerchief, wiped his hands with it while continuing to stare at the unconscious man, and said: "That arm's got to come off."

Enos was staring. "Jack? You know anythin' about this sort of thing?"

Hudson replied, still gazing at Walt Prentice: "A little, Enos. I was hurt in the back durin' the war and ended up helpin' surgeons. Almost two years of it." Hudson pocketed his handkerchief before resuming. "I've helped take off enough arms and legs to make a damned big pile." He paused again, this time to gaze at the other two men before passing his final judgment. "But I'll tell you right now, I've seen 'em like this hundreds of times. He's lost too much blood. The shock will likely kill him."

Enos remained in his chair near the roadway door, but he eased slowly back in it, looking at his helper. It was Redleaf who spoke next. "Could you take the ruined part off, Jack?"

Hudson nodded. "Yes. I've got a satchel of surgical tools in the storeroom across the road." He looked at Orcutt. "Who are his next of kin, Enos?"

Orcutt had no idea. "He never said. In fact, he never hardly ever talked about himself."

"Well, now, Enos, I'm not goin' to take it on myself to amputate that arm. You are his friend. He worked for you. Unless you can come up with

179

a name of someone else around town who was closer to him, it looks to me like you're the one who's got to say yes or no."

Orcutt did not move or speak. He sat, staring at the man who had been his helper, evidently unable even to think about this kind of a responsibility. Hudson looked at Redleaf, and Chet raised and dropped his shoulders. He'd told Enos practically the same thing and had got no more response than Jack Hudson had.

Hudson was not a procrastinator. By nature he was forceful and decisive, and in this situation he was also dispassionate. Not because Prentice had turned out to be an outlaw, but because he privately did not believe Prentice was going to survive with or without the amputation. He had, in

Hudson's view, waited far too long before surrendering.

Enos finally asked if Chet had any whiskey. He had a bottle behind his desk and set it up where the blacksmith could take a couple of long pulls from it. He offered it to Hudson, who declined with a curt head shake as he said: "If we're goin' to do this thing, I'll go hunt up my tools. If we're not, I've got a saloon to run."

Orcutt leaned with both arms on his legs, looking steadily at his helper. The whiskey did not contribute much, if anything, to the decision he finally made. "He'll most likely hate me . . . all of us . . . when he wakes up and finds we taken off one of his arms." Hudson solemnly nodded his head in silence. "But at least he'll be alive," the blacksmith stated. "All right, Jack. Let's take it off."

Hudson turned without a word, slammed the jailhouse door after himself, and walked briskly through the night in the direction of the saloon. Enos had another couple of pulls from the lawman's whiskey bottle, after which Redleaf put it back in the dusty box where he kept it. He did not know whether Hudson would require him and Enos to help in the amputation or not, but if Hudson did require it, the last thing Redleaf wanted was a drunken blacksmith.

Hudson returned fifteen minutes later with a black leather satchel, half an armload of clean towels, some laudanum, and a bottle of whiskey that he placed on Redleaf's table. He rolled up his sleeves past the elbows, washed his hands at the office basin, dried them while gazing at the inert man, and slowly began to scowl as he finished drying his hands.

He approached Prentice, knelt for a long time looking and listening, then straightened back very slowly, looking up. "He's dead."

X

Redleaf rolled Prentice into an old canvas and left him on the storeroom floor, had a pull from his whiskey bottle, skipped supper, and went down to the rooming house tired enough to sleep the clock around. The last two things he'd done at the jailhouse was sluice the office floor with a bucket of water, and bring food from the café to his prisoners. He did not tell them about Walt

Prentice.

The old man who operated the rooming house was friendly for a change as the town marshal came along. He had some questions to ask concerning several things he'd heard, and got no answers as Redleaf closed his door. The whiskey that had seemed to have no effect on Enos a while back had an effect on the town marshal. He slept like a log, did not hear someone rattling his door after midnight, and did not open his eyes until the sun was rising.

He did not anticipate a pleasant new day. For one thing he had to find the local carpenter, have him measure Prentice for a pine box, then muster diggers for the grave hole, and haul the body out there to be put down. For another thing, he was worried about the big Indian who had volunteered to search the mountains for hold-outs who might have witnessed the robbery of that crippled stagecoach. He was also worried about Les Riley whose excursion up to Berksville could have ended up with Les being in trouble up there.

On this last score he need not have worried. The heavy fist that had rattled his door at the rooming house in the wee hours had been Riley. He'd arrived back in Mandan about midnight.

They met at the café but said very little until they were across the road in the privacy of the jailhouse, then Les told Redleaf a lot of things that the lawman already knew, and which Les had coaxed out of the prisoner up in Berksville. Redleaf then told his friend about Walt Prentice, about his prisoners, and, when he had finished, Les made a gesture of resignation. "I'd have done better to stay home," he asserted. Redleaf took him over to the saloon where they drank beer and ate corned beef sandwiches, and that revived Riley's mood a little.

Then Chet told Les about the big Indian, Henry Nye, and Les cocked his head quizzically. "And you want me to go into those damned mountains and find him."

Chet smiled. "No. I doubt that you could. All we can do is wait."

"Hell, you don't need any Indians to identify your prisoners, Chet."

Redleaf nodded. "Yeah. But there's no way I can get that information to Henry Nye."

Riley hunted up the town carpenter

and took him to the jailhouse to measure the corpse while Marshal Redleaf went to see Rod Manion. When he had finished his recitation, the storekeeper, who looked much better than he had looked at their last meeting, stared in wide-eyed astonishment. "Walt Prentice was one of them? I can't believe it. I've waited on Walt at the store dozens of times. He was a nice feller, good-natured and all. And Howard? My God, I'd have trusted him with my life."

As Chet arose to leave, he dryly said: "Maybe Judas Iscariot was a nice feller, too, Rod. I've yet to meet an outlaw who would tell you he wasn't a nice feller. Anyway, they're locked up . . . the live ones . . . and you're lucky they didn't get back down here to roast your toes until you told 'em where your cache is."

"And Henry's in the mountains by himself?"

"Yes."

Manion wagged his head, was still wagging it as Redleaf went downstairs and was waylaid by Manion's tall wife who wanted to know if the rumors going around town were true. He listened to her before agreeing that for the most part, at least as far as the basics were concerned, they were indeed true. He did not tell her about Henry Nye. She already knew about Howard Ballew.

When he got back to the jailhouse, Les and a grizzled, tall, pale-eyed older man were sharing cups of coffee while they waited. When Chet arrived, his friend inclined his head in the stranger's direction and said:

"This here is the U.S. marshal from Albuquerque, Paul Scott."

Chet acknowledged the introduction, eyed the lean, hard-eyed older man, and went after a cup of coffee for himself as he asked what he could do for the stranger, and got back a brusque reply as the hard-eyed older man tossed three folded papers on the table, then sat back, watching Marshal Redleaf unfold them, spread them flat, and read them.

Les Riley, who'd made idle conversation with the stranger until Redleaf returned to the jailhouse, sat straighter in his chair, showing interest, so he clearly had had no previous knowledge concerning the stranger's purpose in being in Mandan. Chet flattened the papers carefully and reread them before raising his eyes to the older man's weathered countenance. The federal officer looked straight back as he said: "They're in order, Marshal. That's the superior court judge's signature on the bottom."

Chet continued to gaze at the hard-eyed man. "I only got them locked up yesterday and you're from Albuquerque. How did you know I had them. Albuquerque is a hell of a distance from Mandan."

The older man made a death's-head smile. "I didn't know until I arrived in town last night and heard the talk at the saloon. I was on my way up north, looking for Ballew, Cuff Waters, and Fred Holden. We got word a couple months back down in Albuquerque that they was somewhere up around Berksville."

"I see. And you were on your way up there?"

"Yep. Looks like you saved me a lot of time, Marshal Redleaf."

Les Riley looked puzzled. "Are those federal warrants, Chet?"

Redleaf looked at the papers under his hands as he nodded. "Yeah. Warrants for Howard Ballew, a man named Holden, a man named Waters. Charges are mail robbery among other things. Federal offences."

Les turned slowly toward the hard-eyed older man and sighed. "Hell of a note. We do all the work and the federal government comes along and takes the prisoners."

The older man laughed. "Except for luck I wouldn't have been able to do it. I was expecting to have to hire a horse up in Berksville country and start hunting for them." He rose and unconsciously adjusted his gun belt. "I've got to eat, then I'll find out when the next southbound stage leaves, and by then, Marshal, you can have 'em ready."

Chet nodded. He and Les watched the older man cross to the door and close it after himself. Les made a little fluttery gesture. "Just like that," he said, sounding annoyed.

Redleaf studied the warrants briefly, leaned back, scratched his head, and put a quizzical gaze upon his friend. "Why just Howard, Cuff, and Fred? That feller you talked to up at Berksville was in with them. So was Walt Prentice."

"Maybe only those three robbed the mail," stated Riley.

Chet got to his feet, crossed to the

cell-room door, and disappeared down the corridor, leaving Les still in his chair where he heard Redleaf ask Fred and Cuff if Brooks and Prentice had been their associates for long. The garrulous outlaw answered.

"Three, four years. They still got Brooks in jail up in Berksville?"

Chet ignored the question. "How about mail robberies, Fred?"

Cuff growled before his companion could reply. "We told you all we're goin' to say. Go ask Walt."

Chet's reply to that shocked his prisoners. "Walt is dead. After I locked you boys in, I went after him. He made a run for it, got shot, and died last night in my office."

Chet did not wait for the shock to pass. He fixed Fred with an unblinking stare as he said: "Who is Paul

Scott?"

Only Ballew's eyes widened. Cuff and Fred looked blank.

He had another question: "Did you rob mail stages using the same system you used to rob the coach with Manion's money on it?"

Fred pushed out a hand to grip one of the steel bars. "We used downed trees across the road or rolled boulders out there. Anything that would force a stage to stop."

Chet studied them from beyond the steel bars. They looked dirtier and more beard-stubbled than they had looked the day before. "Did Brooks and Prentice help at robbing mail stages?"

Fred and Cuff exchanged a look. Cuff shrugged and Fred answered. "Yeah. Prentice did the planning."

Chet hesitated before asking his final question. "Who helped Walt plan the raids?"

The prisoners were silent. Fred returned to the edge of his bunk, sat down, looking at the stone floor. Eventually he said: "All of us worked out the plans."

Chet waited for more, and, when Fred did not add anything, Chet said: "Just you, Cuff, Howard, Walt, and Brooks . . . no one else?"

Not one of the prisoners looked at Redleaf as Fred replied: "No one else."

Cuff nodded his head in verification so Marshal Redleaf returned to the office, closed the cell-room door, and met the faint frown of Les Riley as he crossed to his chair at the table. Les said: "Naw, not the U.S. marshal.

Where'd you get such a crazy idea?"

Redleaf patted the legal documents. "Three warrants, Les."

"They're official, aren't they?"

"Yes. Official blanks that are filled out as they are needed. Les, you heard 'em just now. Prentice, Brooks, and Ballew were with Cuff and Fred when they raided mail stages, but this here U.S. marshal shows up with warrants for the only prisoners I've got. And it was just luck that he happened to arrive in town the day I locked them up. Why didn't he have warrants for Brooks and Prentice? They stole federal mail, too."

A raw-boned man with carroty hair and freckled skin poked his head in from out front to announce that the coffin was ready.

Les went down to the livery barn

for a light dray wagon that he parked in the alley behind the jailhouse. He and Marshal Redleaf carried Prentice out there, then drove across town to the carpenter's shop where the three men fitted Enos Orcutt's defunct helper into the box. The carpenter nailed the lid down.

Les drove back the way they had come, halted behind the saloon, and waited until Marshal Redleaf returned after hiring a pair of local loafers to get their tools and drive out to the Mandan cemetery with Riley and Redleaf and dig a grave.

It was pleasant out there, mostly because the cemetery was shaded by huge old trees. While the diggers worked, Chet and Les leaned in wagon shade, watching. Eventually Les spoke while crushing a tick between his thumbnails. "There were five of them?"

Chet side-stepped a direct reply. "What I know, Les, is that the federal marshals I've had to deal with over the years don't go after a gang of outlaws without all the warrants they'll need. And . . . if they've been keeping track of mail robberies, they know how many highwaymen stopped and robbed stages. This one only talked about the three men I got in my cells."

Les finished squashing the tick and flicked it away. Fifty feet ahead the noise of men digging in soft earth continued. "All right. Now then . . . just who is this man?"

Chet watched the diggers for a while before answering. "I trapped three by following one 'way to hell and gone out where there was to be a rendezvous."

Riley looked around swiftly. "And the other one was already in the *juzgado* up at Berksville. That makes five. Are you saying they were waiting out there for another man?"

"I'm saying, when I crept up on to them they were setting in their camp, talking. Twice they said something about someone named Paul, like he was supposed to show up at the rendezvous, too."

Riley stared. "Paul?"

"Yeah."

Les faced forward to watch the diggers for a while before speaking again. "Naw. No one's that big a damn' fool. If he's one of them, he sure as hell wouldn't use his right name."

Redleaf nodded agreement because the same thought had been troubling him. But there were other discrepancies. He turned to glance back in the direction of town. There was a slight heat haze back there. He could see men in the stage company's corral yard, harnessing a hitch for the southbound stagecoach. He faced forward to watch the diggers briefly, then said: "Let down the tailgate and help me get the coffin out. They can lower Prentice when the hole's deep enough and cover him."

Riley did not say a word until they had the box on the ground and one of the diggers, who had been watching, called to say the hole wasn't deep enough yet. Les called back: "When it is, put the box down in it, cover it, and come back to town!"

The diggers leaned on their shovels, watching Marshal Redleaf and his companion kick off the brakes and turn in the direction of Mandan. One of them tossed aside his shovel, clambered out of the grave, and rummaged in an old coat he'd dropped when the heat and digging had made him sweat. He held up a half-full bottle. The other gravedigger laughed and climbed out to perch on the edge of the grave.

They sat up there in tree shade, passing the bottle back and forth. One of them jerked a thumb in the direction of the pine coffin. "Did you know him?" he asked.

The other man drew a soiled sleeve across his lips before replying. "Yeah. Worked for Enos Orcutt. Seemed like a nice feller, Alfred, except that I got to tell you I always had a feelin' about him."

Alfred turned watering eyes toward his companion. "You never did no such a thing. Every blessed time we come out here and get to talkin' about whoever's in the box, you got to say something like that . . . what're you holdin' your hand out for?"

"Because I'm thirsty, you old screw."

"Here. Now don't hog it, Alfred. You know what your wife used to say."

Alfred handed back the bottle and raised a sleeve to his watering eyes. "What did she use to say?"

"Well, that was before she run off with that drummer with the curly brim derby hat and them spats over his shoes."

"I know who she run off with, for Christ's sake. What did she use to say?"

". . . Who?"

"My wife, for . . . you emptied the bottle, Homer. I got half a notion never to come here an' dig another grave with you. . . . What are you lyin' down for?"

"I'm sleepy."

"Get your scrawny butt up off the grass an' let's finish this hole or we'll miss supper. Get up, Homer."

XI

The U.S. marshal was smoking a long, thin cigar when Redleaf reached the office after leaving Riley to return the hitch and rig to the lower end of town. They exchanged a nod and the federal officer removed his stogie as he said: "There'll be a southbound coach leaving Mandan in half an hour. They told me it was late, but then I've rode darned few stages that was on time."

Chet went to his table, sat down, and put his hat aside. "We just buried Walt Prentice," he said.

Marshal Scott showed no concern. "It happens. Maybe we'd better get them other ones up here in the office and go over them."

Chet did not move. "They don't have any hide-outs."

"Well, I'd like to talk to one of them for a few minutes before we walk up yonder to the corral yard." Marshal Scott smiled through a rising trickle of fragrant blue smoke. "It's my custom, Mister Redleaf, to explain exactly what I expect from them, and what'll happen if they don't do it."

Chet leaned back. "Marshal, do you know how many outlaws were in that band?"

Scott's hard gaze went to Redleaf's face and remained there. "Yeah. You got three of them, one is dead, and I heard in the saloon last night that another one is in jail up at Berksville."

Chet nodded. "Five," he said, and Marshal Scott nodded his head without taking his eyes off Redleaf. "That's the number I come up with," he said.

"You handed me warrants for only three of them."

Scott took a long pull off his cigar before replying. "I knew Prentice was dead and that Brooks was in jail up yonder. That's all they talked about at the saloon last night. Some of those gents were out there when Prentice surrendered to you." For a moment Marshal Scott gazed steadily at Redleaf before slowly removing his cigar to examine the length of ash. As he spoke his voice was different: "You got something bothering you, Mister Redleaf?"

Chet had no opportunity to answer, the door burst open, and Les Riley sprang into the room, looking wild-eyed and breathless as though he had run all the way from the lower end of town. He started to speak, saw the federal officer sitting there, relaxed and comfortable, and checked himself, forced a poor excuse for a smile, and crossed to the stove with his back to the other men to draw off a cup of coffee.

Chet was round-eyed. The federal officer trickled smoke, showed no expression at all, but kept his eyes on Riley's back until Les turned slowly, cup in hand, ignored the federal lawman, and looked directly at Redleaf as he said: "Have you fed your prisoners?"

Chet hadn't. It was slightly past high noon. He hadn't been thinking of that during his conversation with Paul Scott.

"No. In a few minutes. Why?"

Les jerked his head. "Go down there and look," he said.

Redleaf's stomach knotted. He stared steadily at his friend for a moment or two, then rose, took down his copper ring of keys, and hauled back the oaken cell-room door and disappeared in the dinginess as Les Riley put his gaze upon the hard-eyed man across the room from him whose legs were thrust out full length and crossed at the ankles. Paul Scott gazed directly back, smoke lazily rising. He did not remove the stogie but spoke around it. "What's this all about?"

Riley did not reply. Redleaf bellowed from the cell room and came charging back to the office. He said: "They're gone!"

Marshal Scott stopped puffing but otherwise showed nothing and did not move in his chair.

Riley, who had caught his breath and whose agitation had been sustained as long as it could be, nodded at his agitated friend. "Yeah, they're gone. And they had a gun when they ran down the alley to the livery barn. Howard had the weapon. He shoved it into the liveryman's gut. That's how they got three horses." Riley considered his coffee and put the cup aside without having tasted its contents. "They went west from town and headed straight north."

Les faced toward the stove, and turned back with his Colt aimed directly at the federal lawman. Scott's eyes widened slightly, went from the gun to Riley's face, then back to the gun as Riley cocked it. No smoke rose from his cigar. He removed it carefully and shook his head in Redleaf's direction. "You've got an excitable friend. Right now he's out of his mind."

Les's teeth showed in a cold smile.

"While we were out yonder planting Walt Prentice, you were in and out of this office three times. Folks saw you come in and go out. The last time was about fifteen minutes before Howard Ballew shoved a gun in the liveryman's belly." Riley did not take his eyes off the federal marshal. "Chet, let me guess. Those cell doors was unlocked. Maybe it's about time for you to quit hanging your keys on that nail behind your desk."

Paul Scott slowly drew his legs back and began to lean slightly in his chair.

Riley spoke quietly to him. "You come up out of that chair and I'll blow you through the wall."

Scott remained expressionless but his gaze sharpened. "Mister Redleaf," he said, "you better control this idiot before someone gets hurt."

Chet's mind had been working very fast since the discovery that someone had unlocked the cell doors of his prisoners from the outside. For some time now he had been prepared to believe the worst about Paul Scott. But right now he addressed Riley, not Scott, as he began moving around behind Riley and the wood stove in the direction of the cell-room door. He did not draw his weapon until he had the door pulled back, then he wigwagged with the six-gun while simultaneously addressing Scott.

"Reach across with your left hand and drop the gun. Keep both hands in sight."

Finally Scott came up off the chair, looking from one of them to the other. He did not have the chance of a snowball in hell and knew it. Two weapons were aimed at him from a distance of less than thirty feet, and even though only one gun was cocked there was not a gunman living who could draw, aim, cock his weapon, and fire before those other two guns could blow him apart.

He dropped his weapon and shook his head in Redleaf's direction. "You're crazy," he growled.

Chet did not speak; he gestured with his gun barrel and followed Scott down to one of the empty cells, slammed the door on him, jammed the padlock closed, put up his weapon, and said — "You'll have time to think." — and hastened back to the office.

Riley was not there but the roadway door was wide open. Across the road three men burst forth from the saloon with Les Riley out front. One of them had a carbine, the others had only their belt guns. As Riley led his recruits past the pool hall, he bellowed in the doorway. Two pool players dropped their cues and ran outside.

Redleaf went back across his office, pulled the chain through the trigger guards of his racked weapons, took three carbines, and left in a lope heading toward the livery barn. When he got down there, the noise and confusion had attracted other townsmen, but of these onlookers none rushed forth to volunteer, which was probably just as well because by the time Marshal Redleaf had kept one carbine for himself and handed the other two around, men were swinging up across leather.

He led them out into the alley and

northward. The badly upset liveryman had pointed with a rigid arm in
that direction, yelling even after the
posse riders were flinging up the alley. There was more excitement in
town as information of the escape got
around. It was a good thing Chet
Redleaf was not there to hear some
of what was being said.

Jack Hudson from the saloon, along
with Enos Orcutt and the pool-hall
proprietor, went down to the jailhouse, entered the office, saw the
cell-room door ajar, and trooped
down there to gaze with some surprise at the solitary prisoner.

Scott glowered. He told them what
he wanted them to believe, said
Redleaf was crazy, and demanded to
be released. Not a word was said as
the three townsmen turned on their

heels, marched back to the office, carefully barred the cell-room door from the office side, and walked up to the saloon for a drink.

Hudson had served Scott over his bar. The pool-hall proprietor was one of those people who had seen Scott enter the jailhouse several times during Redleaf's absence and Enos Orcutt, the Mandan blacksmith, had been sufficiently benumbed by recent events, including the death of his helper, not to have a whole lot of faith in anyone, particularly if he did not know them, and that disagreeable-acting man locked in one of Redleaf's cells was a perfect stranger to Enos. He was thinking of something else: "How did they unlock their cell door? Chet keeps his key ring on that nail behind his desk.

Hell! Do you expect that's why he locked that feller up? He got the key ring and freed those sons-of-bitches?"

The pool-hall proprietor turned a jaundiced gaze on the blacksmith. "Did you see that feller enter an' leave the jailhouse three or four times while Chet and Les Riley was out at the cemetery? Well, I did. An' I say keep that feller locked up in there until Chet returns an' I don't give a damn whether he's a federal marshal or the President of the United States."

Big, burly Jack Hudson solemnly re-filled three glasses and stoppered the bottle before placing it under his bar top. "They're not goin' to get far," he prophesied. "Chet's got seven men with him an' it don't seem to me those outlaws had that big a head start."

An old gaffer, slumping in a chair beside the unlighted big old cast-iron wood stove, peered from sunken eyes at the other men as he said: "You don't know them mountains or you wouldn't make no such a statement, Jack. All them outlaws need is fast horses an' no more'n a half hour's head start. If they can clear the foothills and get up in there, take my word for it, the devil hisself couldn't find them, tracks or no tracks. I know. I scouted up Indians for Gen'l Miles through them damned mountains for three years."

The old man's statement dampened the grim enthusiasm of his listeners. They had their drinks and left the saloon in silence, all but Jack Hudson, who leaned on his bar top, gazing around his empty place of business, finally settling his eyes upon the ragged old scarecrow slumped in a chair beside the stove. Jack straightened up, filled a shot glass, took it over to the old man, and jerked his head in the direction of the platters of corned beef, coarse bread, and pickles at the free-lunch end of the bar. "Fat up," he growled. "Leave the whiskey here until you've the pleats out of your belly."

The old man raised tired eyes. "I got no money, Jack."

"I wouldn't take it if you did have," the big, burly man growled. "Quit settin' here, feelin' sorry for yourself. Go over there and fill up."

"Jack."

"What?"

". . . If you got a broom, I'll sweep

out for m' food and the whiskey."

Hudson stood a moment, gazing downward. "Did you really scout for General Miles?"

"Yes, for a damned fact. And for a friend of his who didn't have the brains God give a goose. Feller named George Armstrong Custer."

Hudson's eyes widened. "Him, too?"

The old man's eyes crinkled. "Ten years of it. From up along the Canadian line south to New Mexico."

"The Army retired you?"

The old man's mouth pulled wide in a bitter smile. "The Army don't retire nobody under twenty years, an', if it's an enlisted man, he don't get enough to buy a knothole to pee through. For civilian scouts . . . they give you a medal with a pretty ribbon on it and turn you out to grass."

Hudson returned behind his bar when three strangers walked in, beating off dust after a six-hour stage ride. He served them, listened to their grumbling, and, when they departed southward in the direction of the rooming house because there would not be another eastbound stage leaving Mandan until morning, Hudson watched the gaunt old man methodically eating at the free-lunch end of his bar.

He called up to him: "What's your name?"

The answer was barely distinguishable because the old man did not swallow before offering it. "Bud Leslie. I've been in here before. Mostly when it's cold outside."

Hudson nodded. He remembered

the old man but until today had not distinguished him from several other old men without families who huddled around his stove in wintertime, sometimes buying a 5¢ beer, more rarely buying a 10¢ jolt of whiskey. "Bud, I got a proposition for you."

The old man turned his gaunt face with the sunken eyes, chewed, and said nothing.

"There's an iron cot in my storeroom out back. All you can eat. I'll get you some decent pants and shirts down at Manion's store. You wash glasses, keep the place swept out, haul in stove wood in winter. Six dollars a month cash."

The old man chewed, swallowed, pulled a filthy sleeve across his mouth, and turned back to the mammoth sandwich he'd made as he said: "I'll do it, but there's got to be more work'n that, Jack, because I don't take no charity."

Hudson continued to lean and watch the old man. "All right. Keep the backbar dusted an', before you bed down every night, go across the alley and put a shovelful of lye down the holes in the outhouse. I'll think of other things."

Bud Leslie took his sandwich back to the chair by the stove, sat down, and grinned as he reached for the little glass of whiskey. "I bet you will," he said, and dropped the whiskey straight down.

Hudson laughed, swabbed his bar top almost without thought, and, as townsmen began drifting in, he said: "Start first thing in the morning.

When you get through there, go settle in at the storeroom."

XII

Redleaf's riders reached the foothills on sweaty horses. They had fresh tracks that far, so they'd been able to make good time, but there was nothing to see — no movement, not even any dust, which meant the escaping outlaws had not spared their stolen animals to get far enough ahead to be into the timber by the time the townsmen reached the foothills. They took time out to dismount, loosen cinches, roll smokes, and gaze up ahead where tiers of trees, most of which were at least a hundred feet tall, made a place of perpetual gloom as the country sloped steadily upward, in some places almost precipitously upward.

A squinty-eyed thin man with skin like parchment and a prominent Adam's apple that bobbled when he talked raked bent fingers through graying hair and said: "I been pot-huntin' them hills for some years, an' I'm here to tell you that's bad country up there. A man can get lost up there who ain't ever been lost nowhere else."

Les Riley eyed the speaker coolly. "How far back in there have you been?"

The thin man gestured toward the nearest high ridge. "About that far. Maybe six, eight miles." He lowered his arm. "I can guide you that far. But if them renegades went in a different direction. . . ." The thin man spat, shrugged, and remained silent.

When they were astride again, still following gouged tracks left by shod horses digging in with each jump, Redleaf began to suspect that the escaping outlaws had indeed gone in a different direction. They were pushing in among forest giants when the tracks turned eastward paralleling the highest ridge above them.

For a long while nothing was said. Chet read sign in the lead and the others followed him. Once, a posse man, sounding uncomfortable, mentioned the possibility of an ambush that could put them all face down in the dirt. No one replied; it was highly unlikely outlaws, fleeing for their lives, would risk losing the time an ambush would take.

They were crossing a soggy meadow

where mosquitoes arose in the thousands to plague the horses when Chet swung off, retrieved something from the grass, and rode onward while examining it. When he was finished, he passed the object over to Riley and concentrated on reading sign. It was a cracked short length of leather, ragged at both ends where it had torn loose, with a Conway buckle in the middle. It could have come from a cheek piece or perhaps from the length of leather beneath a horse wearing a double-rigged saddle, but one thing was certain — it had not been lying in that damp place very long, otherwise it would have showed rust and the leather would have been soggy, not dry.

Someone made a wry comment. "It come from the liveryman's equipment all right. He never soaped nor oiled a piece of leather in his life."

Redleaf paused on the near side of a gravelly top-out that had been wind-swept down to bedrock in places, handed Les his reins, and crept up to lie flat on the rim. He had an excellent view of the countryside to the east, west, and north. The trouble was that all that magnificent view had varying degrees of timber denseness. It was not possible to see down through to the ground. But what Redleaf was looking for was not on the ground. It originated there but did not stay there — dust.

He saw it higher upcountry north-ward, but eastward as though the fleeing riders were trying to gain height while at the same time hasten-ing eastward. He lay for a long time watching, trying to guess the route of the escaping outlaws, and, when he was satisfied, he returned to the others, who had been squatting in tree shade while their animals rummaged for whatever was edible up here, of which there was precious little because grass did not grow where resin-impregnated pine and fir needles formed carpets six to ten inches deep.

When they were moving again, Chet twisted toward Les Riley directly behind him and said: "What we should have done was go straight up the stage road northward."

"Is that where they're going?"

"Yeah, but my guess is that they'll cross it and keep going eastward. Maybe they know the country over there. If we'd gone up the road, we could have cut them off."

Riley dryly said: "Sure we could have, and, if we had a crystal ball, we could know when it's going to rain."

Shadows began inching around from behind the big trees, frail at first but strengthening as time passed. Redleaf pushed the horses as much as he dared. He did not want to have to call a halt for the night because he did not believe the outlaws would do that.

It was that thin, homely man with the squinted eyes who thought this would not be so. He told the others that no one in their right mind, including outlaws, rode through the night in a damned forest where anything could happen to a man and damned well might happen — even if he wasn't straddling ridden-down saddle stock. Whether this observation was true or false, it put a little heart into the others as Chet finally had to dismount and walk ahead of his animal to make out the tracks because dusk arrived much earlier in stands of big timber than it did where there was no timber.

They reached the stage road, slid their animals down a crumbly embankment to reach the center of it, and halted to listen. The only thing they heard was an invisible animal who had been routed out of its bed by their arrival, and grunted irritably as it fled through the underbrush.

Redleaf rolled and lit a smoke. They were about three hundred yards south of the place where the crippled stagecoach had been forced to halt — and had been robbed. Riley and another man got down to bend close to the ground for tracks. They found them, followed them across to the opposite claybank, straightened up, and gazed at deep gouges where horses had been forced to climb up a very steep bank of soft soil. They told Redleaf where the outlaws had gone and pointed eastward. He nodded absently, picked up his reins, and turned northward up the middle of the stage road. Riley and the man who had scouted with him exchanged a look but said nothing. No one said anything in fact, but they watched Redleaf as men would have done who felt like challenging his decision.

Dusk darkened both sides of the roadbed. Out there, however, there was better light. There were weak stars for a while, until eventually they brightened and coldly blinked, by which time the posse men were riding blind. Redleaf did not lope, did not even lift his horse over into a trot, but he kept riding, so the men behind him did the same. It was a warm night, which was a blessing since most of the riders had flung out of town in such haste they'd had no time to go after coats and jackets.

By the time moonlight added a little to visibility, though, the warmth was fading. Redleaf headed directly toward a gunsight notch in the skyline where the road passed through, halted slightly below it, and swung off to rest the horses. He and Riley walked up to the pass and stood in silence, looking downhill where a fifty-mile swale in the mountain chain ended in the moonlighted dim distance where the country rose up again gradually toward another gun-sight notch. Between one pass and the other there was primitive country. That thin man with the Adam's apple came up behind them and said: "Ain't no different as far as a man can see, but as long as a man stays on the road he'll come out somewhere. If he gets to foragin' around in the trees on either side of the road, he'll get lost sure as hell."

Les turned. "I've freighted this road for a lot of years, friend, and you're right. But Berksville's up there."

"Anythin' in between?"

"Nope. Some grassy meadows you can see through the trees now and then but no settlements of any kind that I ever saw."

The thin man made a laconic observation. "Well, boys, they're up there maybe, an', if they are, they won't be too far ahead. Folks can't abuse saddle stock like they been doin' an' not end up on foot if they don't rest 'em. Nothing's harder on horses than mountainous country. They been pushing those animals like they thought they was made of iron . . . they're up there, gents. From here on it'd pay to ride off the road where the needles will deaden our sound."

It was sound advice, but Redleaf had already decided on a course that was consistent with his idea about the men they were pursuing, and it went back to that earlier robbery of the stagecoach. That time, the outlaws had skulked downcountry parallel to the road on the east side until they found the coach where it had halted. He mounted and turned off the roadway into the easterly timber where it was as dark as the inside of a boot except in rare instances where little grassy glades caught moonlight.

It was Redleaf's opinion that those stage robbers must have had a camp up here somewhere. For that reason, when they came upon one of those grassy places, he would scout around and across it. It was slow going, and, although from time to time they dismounted, looking for shod-horse tracks, they had no success, so they fanned out on foot, leading their animals to form a wide-ranging sweep northward. Redleaf believed as that shrewd, squinty-eyed man believed that the outlaws were somewhere up ahead and probably not too distant. Twice he called a halt, took Les Riley, and scouted ahead on foot.

They found nothing. On the hike after the second scout Chet said they would wear themselves and the horses down doing this. When they got back to the others, he suggested off-saddling, making a dry camp, and getting some sleep. The squinty-eyed man shook his head but said nothing. The others were willing to rest. They would have liked a warming fire but no one suggested it.

The moon soared, stars flickered, occasionally a nocturnal forager rustled fir needles or undergrowth, and the chill deepened. Riley went out to look at the horses and returned to say the squinty-eyed man was gone. There was a little muttering about this, but since the horse he had been riding was still with the other animals the unanimous opinion was that he had gone on a scout.

He had. In fact, when he eventually returned to camp and a drowsy posse man was roused by his presence and challenged him, the lanky man said: "Just settle down, friend. I went for a walk. Back home in Virginia I was raised up walking in the mountains."

His voice roused the other men. They wanted to know if he'd found anything. He answered while moving over where Marshal Redleaf was sitting with his back to a giant red fir tree. "Yes, sir. I found some horses. I didn't go up close. Didn't want them smellin' me and gettin' scairt. Hard to tell from a distance but there was at least three of them in a little park about a mile an' a half ahead down the far side of this here top-out."

Everyone was wide-awake. Les

asked about the riders of those horses but the Virginian's reply was disappointing. "Didn't see hide nor hair of 'em. Didn't find their camp, neither, even though I slunk around lookin' for it. But they got to be over there, boys. That's why I hurried on the way back. We got about two hours more of darkness, then dawn'll come and it'll be too late for us all to sneak back there and set up an ambush. Wherever those gents are hid out among the trees, they sure as hell don't figure to go nowhere without their horses. All's we got to do is get in place and be stonestill when those fellers come out for their animals." The Virginian tapped Redleaf's shoulder lightly. "You're the chief."

Chet rose, popped the stiffness from his legs by flexing his knees, picked up a carbine, and jerked his head. Without a word the others also rose.

The Virginian took the lead. They never lost sight of him, but occasionally his zigzagging route left the others temporarily in doubt.

Les nudged Chet. "Who is he?"

Redleaf did not know the man. "Haven't any idea. I don't recall seeing him around town."

The Virginian stopped beside a huge sugar pine with reddish bark. The others walked right up on to him and might have passed by if he hadn't stepped out in front with an arm raised for silence. He turned and pointed toward a palely lighted clearing of no more than ten acres. There was stirrup-high grass out there and it was still green. At this elevation grass did not turn brown and go to seed until much later than it did at lower elevations.

The posse men crept close to the final fringe of trees that surrounded the grassy place and halted. Riley thought there were five animals over on the far side of the glade. Someone else said it was no more than three horses. That was the number they had expected to find so it was easy to believe there were no more than three animals over yonder. Any more would have made problems for them; the outlaws had escaped from town on three stolen horses. The issue was seemingly resolved when Chet told them to spread out among the trees, some of the men to start circling to the left, the others to start around the meadow on the right. When they were in place, they were to hide and wait for dawn. As soon as the riders of those horses appeared, they were to throw down on them.

The Virginian was smiling broadly; this had been his suggestion. He led off on the left-side surround. Riley led off in the opposite direction, and Marshal Redleaf leaned his carbine against the handsome big sugar pine and hunkered down to wait.

Everything appeared to be progressing satisfactorily until a cougar screamed somewhere southward. The cat could have been close or he could have been farther than he seemed to be, but his scream carried perfectly to those dozing horses. They came awake in a moment and ran in panic toward the center of the glade. Where they halted, milling, unwilling to run in among the trees, Chet Redleaf counted nine horses.

XIII

The horses remained poised to panic, but as moments passed without another scream, they gradually came down from their high and cropped grass, occasionally testing the air for a scent. As time passed even that kind of uneasiness waned.

Redleaf felt like swearing. There was no way the outlaws could have acquired that many horses; he had been on their trail from town and they had not come upon any ranches or any free-grazing ranch animals. He scowled toward where the horses were beginning to spread out as they ate. There was only one explanation

— he and his companions had set up an ambush for men who'd had nothing to do with the jail break. He shoved up to his feet, twisted to brush himself off, and saw the stone-still silhouette of a man not thirty feet distant among the trees.

They regarded each other for a moment before the shadowy silhouette raised a carbine, holding it low in both hands with its barrel aimed squarely at the lawman. It was not a posse man. Even before the weapon came to bear Redleaf sensed something different. After the gun was aimed, he said: "Are those your horses?"

The shadow did not respond. Neither did he look away from Redleaf. To the right where more huge old overly ripe trees hindered visibility a second silhouette appeared and spoke. "You must have a good reason for prowling these mountains in the dark, Marshal."

Henry Nye came soundlessly forward. He had no carbine, just a holstered Colt around his middle. He looked even larger in the gloom.

Chet eased his breath out slowly, looked once again at the first silhouette, then faced the big Indian. "Yeah. We had a jail break. Three of the men who took Manion's box off the stagecoach got set free by another member of the gang, and came up here, riding hell for leather."

Nye thought about that for a while before asking a question. "You got 'em dead to rights?"

"Yes. If I'd known how to contact you, I'd have done it. We won't need any Indians to identify them."

Henry Nye glanced in the direction of the statue-like silhouette. "Come on over here, Owl."

The silhouette was a lean young Indian whose attire was about equal parts white man's clothing and tanned deerskin. He grounded his Winchester while looking straight at Redleaf, and neither spoke nor nodded as he was introduced to the lawman.

Henry Nye rubbed the tip of his nose while gazing at the young buck. He told him about the fleeing outlaws and the Indian grinned, showing perfect white teeth in the chilly predawn. Chet asked Henry Nye if the Indian thought it was amusing that he and his posse men had ridden themselves to a frazzle in pursuit of outlaws.

Nye shook his head, looking bemused. "No. But in the middle of the night someone in the camp heard horses whinnying and roused the others. They scattered through the timber on foot. Some of them saw three riders going past at a dead walk on very tired horses."

The Indian said: "White men."

Nye nodded. "White men."

Chet was interested. "In which direction?"

"North," stated the big Indian, and shifted position a little. "Where are your friends, Marshal?"

Redleaf gestured. "Around the clearing waiting to catch someone coming out after those horses."

"It might be a good idea to leave them out there for the time being."

Henry Nye jutted his chin in the Indian's direction. "These folks would just as soon as few people as possible knew they are up here." Nye switched his attention to the Indian. "Do you suppose you could take a few men, find where those outlaws are camped, and steal their horses?"

Again the buck broadly smiled. "Yes. Will you keep these men away from the camp?"

Nye nodded his head, and the Indian faded out among the trees.

Nye got comfortable on the ground, gazing out where those nine horses were eating. "You're wondering how I found these people. Well, I didn't find them, they found me. I was bumbling around north of here a few miles. It was getting dark, so I made camp near a little creek, slept like a dead man, and in the morning, when I opened my eyes, there they were. Six of them, sitting there like a row of rocks with blankets around them." Nye grinned. "I invited them to breakfast. Of the six three could not speak English. They were the older men. The younger men, like Owl who was one of them, all spoke English."

Chet had a question. "If they're so shy about folks knowing they are up in here, why didn't they just let you ride on?"

"Curiosity. By the light of dawn they could see my hide was about the same color as their hide. If I'd been a white man, they would have let me ride past." Nye paused to look at Redleaf. "They need friends, Marshal. They have a main camp about seven miles northwest of here beneath a big granite over crop. It's in a beautiful big meadow, a regular picture-postcard setting. They need many things. Medicine, for example, woolen blankets, warm clothing that is better than split-hide shirts and britches. They need iron cooking pots, gunpowder, and lead. It tugs at a man's heart to see how they live, as wary as coyotes, always fearful someone will see them and tell the Army where they are." Henry Nye squinted eastward where a feeble paleness was beginning to appear. "I'm not going to say I saw any hold-outs up here." He turned questioning dark eyes on Redleaf.

Chet was agreeable. "Nor am I."

Nye accepted that. "Then all we got to worry about is your posse men." He brushed himself off as he stood up. Chet also got to his feet. Nye gestured in the direction of the fish-belly sky. "If you'll round them up, Marshal, and take them back the way you came to that boggy meadow down there, I'll deliver their horses to you and with any luck the outlaws, too." Nye looked long at Marshal Redleaf. "It's got to be done without the outlaws seeing the Indians."

Chet turned to watch the horses briefly. "How do you do that, Mister Nye? Those outlaws know someone is behind them. I think they only have one gun among them, but, if I'm wrong, someone could get killed."

Nye looked thoughtful. "I wouldn't pretend to know how these people stalk wild game and kill it with rocks, but I know for a fact they do it. I'd say your outlaws wouldn't be too much trouble for them." Henry Nye shoved big hands deep into trouser pockets and changed the subject. "How is Rod Manion?"

"Much better. Did you know the feller who clerked for him at the store?"

"Yes. Ballew, wasn't it?"

"He was one of the band who robbed the coach. He's one of the outlaws your Indians will be after. Another one was the town blacksmith's helper. He's dead. There was another one we didn't know about until he showed up pretending to be a federal lawman, and turned loose Ballew and the pair of men with him out yonder somewhere."

Nye said: "You've been busy, Marshal."

Redleaf watched the big man moving among the trees, lost sight of him, and lifted his hat vigorously to scratch. He did not dwell upon the unique meeting or the big Indian's concern for the hold-outs; he concentrated instead on how he was going to convince his posse men they should go back down to that mosquito-inhabited wet meadow.

He started around the horse meadow southeastward, which was the direction Les Riley had taken. The dawn was cold; there was not a sound. Evidently roosting birds had detected the presence of men down below and had left the area. Those Indian horses seemed not to have picked up man scent, or, if they had, they were indifferent to it.

Les Riley rose twenty feet in front of Redleaf where he had been sitting in a wild grape thicket. He yawned, then said: "They should have come out here by now."

Chet looked elsewhere among the trees and undergrowth as he spoke. "Someday I'll tell you why we are going back down to that wet meadow, but not right now. Can you find the others?"

Les stared for a moment before answering. "Yeah. But they've put in a lot of time on this manhunt, Chet. They're going to want to know why we're going back empty-handed."

"Tell 'em the outlaws cut back."

"Did they?"

Redleaf continued to avoid his friend's gaze. "They could have. Round up the others and meet me back where we left the horses."

Riley watched the lawman passing

back among the trees and spat, hitched at his britches, and turned to find the other posse men.

The sun was rising by the time Redleaf's companions came around the clearing to where he was waiting. That Virginian with the Adam's apple asked Chet pointblank if he knew for a fact that the men they were hunting had cut back.

Even Les Riley stood motionlessly awaiting Redleaf's reply. Chet's answer was curt. "They lost their horses, and being livery animals my guess is that the animals will start back."

The Virginian squinted. "An' you figure they'll try to track 'em down and catch them?"

"Something like that. Let's get mounted up."

The Virginian did not move. "Marshal, I'd like to know how you know them bastards lost their horses."

Chet answered while moving toward their saddle stock. "I heard horses going south last night. It wasn't those animals out yonder and it wasn't our horses, so that left the other ones."

The Virginian seemed to accept that. So did the other men, at least until they'd been on the trail for a while with sunlight beginning to bring warmth into the new day, then a raffish red-headed man eased up beside Riley and said: "This don't make sense to me. If they lost their horses, then seems to me we should be gettin' between them fellers on foot to keep them from finding their damned horses, an' that way we'd maybe catch 'em."

Riley did not argue. His response was offered tiredly. He did not understand this any better than the others did, but he had faith in Chet Redleaf. "If the marshal wants to do it this way, friend, then I guess we'll do it this way. All I give a damn about is that we find those men."

The red-headed man may not have been satisfied with that explanation, but he reined back and rode along, looking more bewildered than annoyed.

It was the Virginian who kept the topic alive. He was evidently garrulous by nature, and, with something he did not understand bothering him, he alternated between periods of loquacious complaining and scowling silence. Redleaf ignored them as he led the withdrawal back down through the timber. He was less worried about what they thought than he was about the possibility that Henry Nye might not be able to deliver the stolen horses and the men who had stolen them. If he failed, Redleaf was not only going to have a lot of explaining to do, but he was going to have to do it without mentioning Indians, and that, he told himself, presented the most difficult decision of his life — whether to tell the truth or to manufacture the biggest lie he had ever told.

When they reached the vicinity of the sump meadow, the sun was well aloft even though it did not penetrate the forest in very many places, and, while there was warmth, it was less than the sun's heat would be out in open country.

They did not go very close to the wet meadow because of the mosquitoes, but they were bothered by the hungry little insects even then. Until the heat eventually arrived, they were occupied in making big sweeps with their hats to prevent being bitten. The horses used manes and tails and stamping feet to protect themselves against all but the boldest mosquitoes. Gradually the insects abandoned the shadows and returned to the meadow. Their reason was a large band of deer that had come out of the northward forest in search of soft grass and water.

Chet lighted a smoke as did everyone else who smoked. Mosquitoes did not like any kind of smoke. Eventually the posse men had sufficient relief to turn their attention to other things. Riley and the Virginian took the horses farther back in search of a grassy place. When they returned without the animals, the Virginian appeared to have been lectured about pestering Marshal Redleaf; at any rate he settled on the ground with his saddle for a pillow, tipped an old hat over his face, and went to sleep without saying a word. The other men also stretched out. They had been cold last night. They had not slept. This seemed to be an excellent opportunity to emulate the Virginian.

Les came over and dropped down near Redleaf. He rolled and lit a smoke and raised questioning eyes. "You got a good reason for this?" he asked.

Redleaf's answer was rueful. "It'd

better be. If it's not, I might just as well saddle up and leave the country."

Les trickled smoke. "Indians?" he said casually.

Redleaf blinked. "What made you say that?"

"Those horses back up yonder. I was setting in the bushes real still and a couple of 'em came along, picking grass. Indian horses, Chet. One had cropped ears, the other one had somethin' braided into a few strands of his mane right up behind his ears. I couldn't make it out, but I've seen Indians' horses before that had those little braids."

Redleaf glanced among the trees where the posse men were either dozing or sleeping. "Henry Nye was up there."

"The hell!"

"Came out of the trees. There was a young buck, too. Nye said the Indians would try to capture the outlaws, but whether they could do that or not, they will steal their horses and bring them down here. I agreed to make a trade with them . . . they either catch the outlaws or set them afoot, and we'd come down here and wait."

Riley stubbed out his smoke. "Well, if they do it, that's not going to keep that feller from Virginia and the others from wondering how it happened."

Redleaf had already considered this and it bothered him less than what the outlaws would have to say about how they had been captured. "I don't know what Nye had in mind except for setting those men on foot. But I do know that, if he delivers Cuff, Fred, and Howard down here, it's not going to be any secret that they were caught by hold-outs, and that kind of talk will eventually reach the Army. All I promised was not to say I'd met any Indians up there."

Riley stood up and yawned. The heat was increasing even in the depth of the forest. "You don't have to worry about me saying anything. As far as I'm concerned, they can have this kind of country and more power to 'em." Les paused, gazing down at his friend. "How in hell do you get yourself into messes like this?"

For the first time in the new day Redleaf smiled. "I work real hard at it."

Riley turned to peer out through the timber in the direction of the soggy meadow. "Maybe it'd be a good idea if someone kept watch out there. It'd be a hell of a note if Nye's redskins brought those bastards down here and we were all asleep."

Redleaf agreed. "Yeah. That's my job."

"I can spell you off. I'll nap for a while, then spell you."

Chet nodded, and the freighter went back through the trees.

A band of blue jays came winging into the treetops, saw the men down below, and started their customary noisy caterwauling, which served as a warning to other upland wildlife that trespassers had invaded their area. Maybe the other creatures heeded the squawking, but the posse men didn't — except for Redleaf, who rose to pace among the trees because sitting still made him drowsy.

XIV

The Virginian awakened, raised his hat to look around, then sat up as Marshal Redleaf moved past. "Marshal, you hear anything?"

Chet stopped. "No."

The lanky mountaineer rolled over, lowered his head with an ear to the ground, remained like that briefly, then sat up squinting. "I guess I felt it," he said, and got to his feet.

Redleaf frowned. "Felt what?"

"Put your ear to the ground, Marshal. It's horses coming."

"From what direction?"

The Virginian raised a long arm. "Sort of northeast, I think. Listen."

Chet heard them, but very faintly. They did not appear to be traveling fast. In fact, if it had been only one horse, he probably would not have made enough noise to be heard, but it sounded like several horses.

He went among the men, rousing them. The Virginian stood a while listening, then faded back among the trees. He gestured for everyone else to do the same, and they did.

Les Riley reached inside his shirt to scratch as he watched the far side of the meadow. The sounds were clearly audible now. Les said: "I thought they'd be hightailing it."

No one commented.

It was not a long wait, but it seemed to be, before they could see movement over through the timber. Redleaf leaned against a large tree, relieved that Henry Nye's tomahawks had been able to steal the horses, and slightly disappointed when he could finally see all three animals because they were not carrying riders.

Riley noticed this, too. "Now we've got their animals, we can go back up yonder and hunt them down. You want to know something, Chet. I've been hungry so long my belly thinks my throat is cut."

One of the posse men wordlessly offered Riley a gnawed square of molasses-cured cut plug. Les looked at it, shook his head, and, as the posse man was pocketing the plug, Les shuddered. Just once he'd tried chewing tobacco. He'd been so sick he had thought he would die and had wished to hell he could.

That inquisitive red-headed older man hissed: "Yonder. See 'em? Three bays."

The horses stopped at the edge of

the meadow, lowered their heads, and greedily cropped grass. The red-headed man muttered. "Wait. Them mosquitoes'll be along."

He was right. The starved animals began swinging their tails, shaking their manes and stamping, but not even biting mosquitoes could make them leave the meadow. Someone behind Chet in forest gloom muttered that it was a damned shame to treat animals the way those horses had been treated.

The animals were in full view across the little meadow. While they stood back in the semidarkness watching them, the Virginian said: "Couple of us could take ropes an' sneak around to that side and most likely either catch them or spook them on southward toward town."

Riley answered that. "Just shut up and wait," he growled. "Unless I'm wrong as hell, those outlaws will be tracking them because they can't get horses anywhere else."

That seemed to settle it for the Virginian as well as for the other posse men. Several knelt to get comfortable. The red-headed man had a question for Redleaf: "Marshal, if you heard them horses passin' southward last night, why do you expect it took them this long to get down here?"

Chet sighed. "They were hungry and most likely they had no reason to run all the way. Free-ranging horses sometimes take forever just to go five miles. You ought to know that, if you been around horses very much."

The red-headed man was rebuffed

and remained silent. He was the one who had offered Riley chewing tobacco to take the edge off his hunger.

The horses were gradually grazing out toward the middle of the meadow, ravenously eating grass and fighting mosquitoes. If they hadn't been starved, they wouldn't have remained out there for ten minutes, not with clouds of stinging insects hovering above them.

Suddenly three men appeared among the farthest trees. They walked forth, then halted, wary as wolves but clearly anxious about the grazing horses. They were motionless for a long time before one of them, a burly, muscular man, stepped in front of his companions into the sunlight, swung his head, then said something as he walked out into plain sight of the motionless watchers across the glade. He had a bridle draped from one shoulder.

Redleaf looked at Riley. "Fred," he murmured, "the one that fake U.S. marshal said was named Fred Holden."

Les nodded without speaking. He was intently watching the other two who were still obscured by forest gloom.

Fred was attacked by mosquitoes, pulled his hat off, and swung it. This time, when he spoke, the hidden watchers heard profanity. Finally the other men stepped into the sunlight, splitting off to approach the grazing horses from both sides. Chet straightened up off the tree he'd been leaning against, and the Virginian said: "Now we can sidle around through the trees and come up behind 'em, Marshal?"

Redleaf shook his head in silence without taking his eyes off the outlaws. By sunlight he recognized every one of them. Several of the posse men murmured when they recognized Manion's store clerk.

The horses sidled away. They did not throw up their heads and flee, but they moved away each time one of the outlaws started easing up to them.

Les Riley knelt and raised his Winchester to track the preoccupied outlaws who were softly talking their way closer to the horses. The red-headed posse man also knelt, so did the Virginian.

Redleaf grunted to himself. The outlaws on both sides and behind the loose stock were inadvertently driving the animals directly across the meadow toward him.

The loquacious Virginian softly said: "This is goin' to be like shootin' fish in a rain barrel."

Redleaf growled at him: "Don't you even cock that gun."

The Virginian removed his thumb from the hammer.

Out in the sunlight the outlaw called Cuff was chumming his way up to one of the bay horses. He had his back to the invisible posse man when he called to his companions. "Slow! Slow 'n' easy. I got this one about caught."

The animal had a gutful of grass. With his hunger appeased, he stood like a docile cow and allowed Cuff to stroke his neck, working forward from the withers until he could loop a rein around the horse's neck. He waited a moment before easing up his left hand to place the bit into the horse's mouth. His companions watched without moving until Cuff had bridled the bay horse and led it over close to the remaining loose animals, then Ballew and Fred moved in.

They had their horses. While the bridling was being done, the store clerk said: "I'd have given a lot of money to have had a rifle when those damned bears spooked them."

Fred was, as always, philosophical. "The hell with the bears, we got 'em back."

Marshal Redleaf waited until the last throat latch was buckled, then raised his Winchester in both hands, holding it belt buckle high, and walked out of the timber into filtered daylight.

The outlaws were turning to lead the horses eastward when Redleaf called to them: "Drop the reins and stand still!"

The outlaws stopped in their tracks. Only Fred twisted to look across the meadow. Riley walked forth as did the other posse men, all of them with fisted guns. Fred sighed and slowly opened his hand to let the reins drop. He spoke quietly to his companions but the words carried. "There's a whole damned army of 'em."

Cuff, the highly strung outlaw, fidgeted before slowly facing around. Howard Ballew neither looked around nor dropped the reins, but his shoulders sagged.

Marshal Redleaf hardly raised his voice as he said: "Which one of you has the gun? Toss it down."

Ballew had it shoved in the front of his britches. He obeyed the order but still would not look around.

Riley lowered his carbine, looked around for the Virginian, and jerked his head. Those two went off westward back through the timber to the grassy place where they had left the horses earlier.

Chet told the outlaws to turn around and walk toward him, and bring the horses with them.

A posse man said: "Hell, I never figured it'd be this easy."

Chet made a muttered reply: "We're not back to town yet."

When the outlaws halted about thirty feet away, they ranged looks among the posse men, then regarded Marshal Redleaf in stony silence. He sent two posse men to go over his prisoners for hide-outs although he did not expect them to have any, nor did they.

They looked tucked up and drawn out. Cuff and Howard were thoroughly dispirited and had every right to be. Fred hooked thumbs in his waistband, wagged his head, and said: "You'd never have caught us if it hadn't been for them damned bears. They come in the dark and scairt the pee out of the horses."

Chet studied the outlaw, the only one of them he did not actively dislike. "Bears," he quietly said. "How many?"

"Hell, we don't know, but there was more'n two or three of 'em. They come out of the trees straight for the horses."

Chet nodded. Bears did not travel in packs, nor would they go anywhere near an area that had the sour scent of human beings in it, let alone deliberately stalk horses where there was man smell.

Riley and his companion returned, leading the posse horses. It did not take long to rig out and get astride for the ride back to lower country. The outlaws had to ride bareback, but that was the least of their problems. Because of the forest, Chet had his prisoners ride one behind the other in the middle of the column with posse men in front and behind them. He had no intention of losing them again.

Once or twice the men talked, but

mostly they followed Chet through the timber on the downslope side in silence. When they could see sun-bright range land through the trees, Redleaf guessed it had to be about midday. He could not see the sun for another hour, by which time it was slanting away from the meridian. And it was hot when they finally rode clear of the uplands, starting down through the rolling low foothills in the direction of Mandan.

Spirits brightened a little when the men left the gloom behind. There was some talk of eating a horse, sleeping for a week, and even taking an all-over bath. The prisoners did not enter into the conversation until they had rooftops in sight, by which time it was midafternoon.

Mandan's tree shade was a respite

after the long ride across treeless range land. Chet avoided the main roadway, halted out behind his jailhouse, herded his captives inside, locked them into the same cells they had previously occupied, which was beside the cell of their friend, the imitation U.S. marshal, and left them there.

As he was walking back toward the office, Fred called after him. "When do we eat?" Chet closed the heavy door, barred it from the office side, and went over to the water bucket, which others had half emptied.

The posse men took the horses down to the livery barn, then split up, half aiming for the café, the others aiming for Jack Hudson's saloon.

Les Riley sank into a chair at the jailhouse office and let go a rattling long sigh. "I've been keeping track. At a dollar a day you owe me about ten dollars."

Chet's eyes widened. "We haven't been after them for ten days."

Riley remained unperturbed. "Did you ever hear of something called overtime? That's what they pay on the railroad and in cities when you work a man past eight or nine hours a day. I said I've been keeping track."

Chet leaned back. "We're not through yet. We got the thieves but we didn't get Manion's money."

Les scowled. "Where is it?"

"I don't know. I'll get Howard up here and maybe he can tell us. But I'll make a guess. It's cached somewhere between here and that place where they camped up in the mountains."

Riley sat morosely until Redleaf returned with the store clerk, pushed him down on a wall bench, and asked pointblank where was Rodney Manion's $4,000?

Ballew was reluctant to answer until Riley leveled a finger at him. "Let me tell you something, Howard. If I've got to ride back up into the mountains again to find your cache, I'm going to come back and break your neck. And I'm not threatening you. I'm making you a promise." Riley lowered his hand. "And I'll tell you something else. I'm a freighter. I drive horses and mules from a wooden seat. You know why? Because I hate to ride 'em."

The store clerk considered Riley's angry face for a moment before switching his attention to Marshal

Redleaf. "We been talkin' among ourselves. We got what you want and you've got the keys to let us out of here in the middle of the night."

Chet rocked forward to lean on his table. "Not on your damned tintype, Howard. The only two things I want now is Manion's money and for the circuit rider to get to town and sentence you bastards to prison and get all of you out of my sight. Now, one more time . . . where is Manion's money?"

The store clerk hunched forward, studying his hands. Riley shifted on his chair, gathered both legs, and gripped the chair with his hands, looking balefully across the room. He was ready to hurl himself at the man on the wall bench.

Ballew raised his eyes. "It's hid in a

pouch behind Manion's desk at the store."

Redleaf stared. "Across the road?"

"Yes." Ballew saw their astonishment and straightened up on the bench. "That was Paul Scott's idea. I was to take it back to town after we got it, and hide it. Later, when the excitement died down, I was to fetch it to a meeting place. Paul didn't trust Cuff and Fred."

"But he trusted you?"

Ballew nodded. "We're related. We worked together a lot."

Chet's brows dropped. "That's his real name? Paul Scott?"

"Yeah, that's his real name. Why shouldn't it be?"

"Because I overheard you fellers up at your rendezvous mention a Paul Scott, so I knew the name before he showed up."

Ballew nodded. "Yeah. But we didn't know that. We didn't know you was out there listening."

Redleaf rose to take a pair of leg irons off a hook with which he chained Howard Ballew to the wall bench. He stood a moment, gazing downward, then jerked his head for Riley to follow him. As they were leaving the office, Redleaf said: "Go ahead and get loose, if you can. Those irons have held a lot of men."

Enos Orcutt was emerging from the café as Redleaf and Riley crossed the road. Chet beckoned to him, did not say why as he entered the General Store and, under the testy gaze of Manion's tall wife and another older woman who was having a list filled, marched back to the storekeeper's dingy office, walked in, and gestured for Riley and Orcutt to get on the far end of the massive old oak desk, and lift.

They could not lift the desk. It was too heavy for that, so they gruntingly see-sawed it until Redleaf could look behind it. There was a stained old canvas money pouch back there. He fished it out, using a long pole, opened it atop the desk, and, with the town blacksmith looking speechless, packets of greenbacks tied with red string tumbled out.

From the doorway someone gasped. Chet did not look around as he began stuffing the money back into the pouch, but Manion's wife moved resolutely forward and stopped the marshal with a firm grip on his wrist. The three men watched her lean down and examine the little packets, pick up several for a closer inspection, then hand them to Marshal Redleaf. "Is it the same money?" she asked.

Chet went back to filling the pouch. "Yes. Howard Ballew's over in the jailhouse. He told us where he'd hidden it."

Manion's wife reached with a firm hand, took the pouch from Redleaf, nodded brusquely, and marched out of the office. Up until now the blacksmith had not said a word, but, as the tall woman departed, he sank down upon Manion's desk chair and groaned. "It was here in town all the time? What kind of damned sense does that make?"

Redleaf's reply was as dry as an old cornhusk. "Pretty good sense, Enos.

Stage robbers ride like hell after a theft, and lawmen go after them. Who would ever think to look in the very store of the man the money was stolen from? Come along, Les. We'll lock Howard in his cell and go get something to eat."

They left the blacksmith sitting there, looking bewildered. As they were approaching the café, Les said: "Finding the money like that was a blessing. I would have sworn we'd have to go back up yonder and maybe move a ton of boulders to find it."

Jack Hudson and the liveryman were already at the counter, eating. They looked up, nodded, and, as Redleaf and Riley sat down, the liveryman leaned around the barman to ask if what he'd heard at the saloon was true, that Chet and Les had brought in the escaped outlaws, plus one other outlaw who had already been locked in one of his cells. Redleaf looked down at the liveryman, ignored the question, and asked one of his own. "What d'you call that big mare of yours that I've been riding lately?"

The liveryman hung fire. He had not expected the question. "Sometimes I call her You Old Bitch, sometimes I call her Sow, and sometimes. . . ."

"How much do you want for her?"

The liveryman's eyes flickered to the barman before he answered. "Marshal, you don't want to ride no mare. They're. . . ."

"How much!"

"I don't like mares. I never liked mares. Thirty-five dollars and I'll throw in the halter."

"Thirty dollars and you keep the halter."

"Done. Mind if I ask a question?"

"Yeah, I mind. I'm hungry right now. I'll be down to pay you sometime before evening."

Jack Hudson had enjoyed the exchange. He finished eating, dropped coins beside his platter, arose, and slapped Redleaf on the shoulder and walked out, leaving the liveryman sitting there in dogged silence to finish his meal alone.

Riley left after supper to visit the tonsorial parlor, rent a towel, the use of the bathhouse out back, and a bar of brown soap. Redleaf took pails of stew across the road, refused to talk to his prisoners, left the buckets under their cell doors, and returned to his office to roll and light a smoke, and to sit down on something that wasn't moving without having to listen to anyone or talk to anyone as daylight waned.

It was a short respite. Rodney Manion burst in, looking exuberant. He launched into a lengthy exclamation of gratitude that Redleaf listened to while smoking. When Manion was finished, Chet said: "Rod, I owe Les Riley fifteen dollars for the time he put in helping me round up the thieves and get your money back."

Manion flinched, then drew forth a wallet, unsmilingly counted out the greenbacks, placed them on Redleaf's table, and without another word or even a nod walked out, slamming the door after him.

Chet gazed at the closed door.

"That's why people like you," he said to the departed visitor. "Because you're so generous and decent and all. You tight-fisted old son-of-a-bitch."

He settled back in the faint gloom of oncoming dusk, cocked his feet atop the table, and finished his cigarette. He was close to dozing when the roadway door opened again, but this time the visitor filled the opening, almost over-filled it. He nodded across the room, removed his hat, and beat clouds of dust from his clothing. As he was doing this he said: "Satisfied, Marshal?"

Chet smiled. "Yup. Plumb satisfied. Tell me something, Mister Nye. How many bears were up there, scaring those horses?"

The large Indian eased down into

the chair Les Riley had vacated earlier. "None."

"I didn't think so."

Nye pushed out thick legs and
eased back in the chair. "They have
tanned bearskins with the hair on
they use for some kind of hunting
ceremony. To keep them believable,
they rub bear scent on them each
time they kill a bear to eat." Nye's
dark eyes twinkled. "It worked. The
horses left in a hurry, and, after they
shed their bearskins, the tomahawks
sort of eased the horses around until
they smelled that green grass and
water. Pretty clever, Marshal. Your
outlaws did not see an Indian, and as
far as I was concerned . . . and they
were concerned . . . that was what
mattered most. Incidentally they hid
out and watched you capture your

outlaws." Nye shifted position in the chair. "Would you say that maybe you owed those Indians, Marshal?"

Redleaf saw the big man's eyes resting on the $15 Manion had left on his table. He sighed, leaned, and pushed it to the edge of the table. "I'd say I owe them, Mister Nye. Will that help?"

Henry Nye's huge paw closed around the money as he stood up, smiling. "It surely will, Mister Redleaf. In the morning I'm going to take a pack string up there with supplies."

Chet cocked his head a little. "You better tell Manion it's supplies for the mine you two are going to work on. He doesn't like Indians very much. Well, hold-out Indians anyway."

Nye went to the door and smiled. "Odd thing about people, Mister Redleaf, they don't like one another unless there is a way they can make money off each other. You ever wonder about that?"

Chet shook his head. "Nope, never have. But it's something to think about. Good luck, Mister Nye." The large man winked and left the office.

Chet fished around for his whiskey bottle, had a couple of swallows, and locked up from out front before heading for the rooming house. Tomorrow it would be something else.

ABOUT THE AUTHOR

Lauran Paine who, under his own name and various pseudonyms has written over a thousand books, was born in Duluth, Minnesota. His family moved to California when he was at a young age and his apprenticeship as a Western writer came about through the years he spent in the livestock trade, rodeos, and even motion pictures where he served as an extra because of his expert horsemanship in several films starring movie cowboy Johnny Mack Brown. In the late 1930s, Paine trapped wild horses in northern Arizona and even, for a time, worked as a professional farrier. Paine came to know the Old West through the eyes of many who had been born in the previous century, and he learned that Western life had been very different from the way it was portrayed on the screen. "I knew men who had killed other men," he later recalled. "But they were the exceptions. Prior to and during the Depression, people were just too busy eking out an existence to indulge in Saturday-night brawls." He served in the U.S. Navy in the Second World War and began writing for Western pulp magazines following his discharge. It is interesting to note that all of his earliest novels (written under his own name and the pseudonym Mark Carrel) were published in the British market and he soon had as strong a following in that country as in the United States. Paine's Western fiction is characterized by strong plots, authenticity, an apparently effortless ability to construct situation and character, and a preference for building his stories upon a solid foundation of historical fact. *Adobe Empire* (1956), one of his best novels, is a fictionalized account of the last twenty years in the life of trader William Bent and, in an off-trail way, has a melancholy, bittersweet texture that is not easily forgotten. In later novels like *Cache Cañon* (Five Star Westerns, 1998) and *Halfmoon Ranch* (Five Star Westerns, 2007), he showed that the special magic and power of his stories and characters had only matured along with his basic themes of changing times, changing attitudes, learning from experience, respecting Nature, and the yearning for a simpler, more moderate way of life.

DATE DUE

GB	DHe,	3601	2115
D.B!³	DWL	GB	
NH			
JWS			
DR			
+3			

Demco, Inc. 38-293